The Second Phase

San Ika

ISBN: 1494906872
ISBN-13: 978-1494906870

The 'Minuet' ringtone on the Smartphone disrupted Rakesh's slumber for the second time in four hours. If he included the 'Timba', the tone for the alarm, which had gone off at six am, the latest disruption transpired as the third. Perplexed as to why he had received the unsolicited wake-up call on a Saturday morning despite the fact he had set the alarm only for weekdays, Rakesh turned to check the time on the phone's docking station. This docking accessory served as nothing more than a clock ever since his employer upgraded his phone - another victim of a strategically planned obsolescence. The big bold numbers displayed 10.18 am. As he took note of the hour of the day, Rakesh grabbed the still ringing phone with a lethargic enthusiasm, and noticed a number with an area code of 248. Unable to recognize the caller, he let the voicemail handle what it did best.

A couple of minutes later, with an abundance of reluctance and laziness, he pulled himself off the bed, stretched, walked over to the window, and parted the beige fabric vertical blinds. Rakesh peered out to verify the accuracy of the highly paid WDXZ Channel Six weather forecaster.

The six-foot bay window of his bedroom overlooked a sizeable acreage of woods which served as a common area of his condominium complex - the Maple Valley Condominiums. Rakesh had not yet discovered a single valley on the terrain of the condo, although Maple trees were in abundance and made up the bulk of the woods. Beyond was Rosemary Road, a major thoroughfare replete with every conceivable element of a well-established metropolitan commercial area. Once the trees shed their leaves in autumn, the Mobil gas station at the intersection of Rosemary and Maple road became visible, along with the endless busy traffic. Mercifully, the noise of the urbanism remained negligible all year long from within Rakesh's home.

True to the weather prediction from the previous night, the ground of the common area was covered with a fresh coat of overnight snow, punctured only by the markings of the nocturnal critters. While the surface was bright white, the sky remained dull gray with overcast clouds. The forecast had also included a partially sunny day for this Saturday on December 8th. Well, so far, the sun could be seen nowhere, partial or otherwise.

As he stared into the snowy oblivion, Rakesh recalled not hearing the 'Calypso' on his phone which would have indicated a yet-to-be-attended voicemail. Upon further cursory scrutiny of the phone, he found the two missed calls but no voicemails from either one. As he fiddled with the call history, he recognized the first caller as one of his friends while the second one remained a mystery other than the number itself. Without further thought, he assumed the unknown caller to be a local telemarketer who, out of bounds from the norm, actually had the etiquette to openly disclose his or her numerical identity.

Only a few minutes elapsed before the phone rang again. The mystery caller was back. With an elevated level of inquisitiveness, Rakesh answered.

A female voice spoke with a hesitating tone. "Hi, uh, can I speak with, uh, I hope I am saying the name right, uh, Rakesh?"

"This is he."

"Oh, hi, hope I didn't catch you at the wrong time. Do you have a moment?"

Unsure of the identity or the intent of the caller, Rakesh uttered a tentative 'Uh-huh' as an attempt to acknowledge the female's question.

"Well, you probably don't remember me by now. My name is Lina and…"

Of course Rakesh remembered Lina. How could he ever forget? It had just been about a month. Startled and surprised at the fact Lina had decided to call, Rakesh interrupted her and blurted out, "Oh gosh, I do remember you. How have you been, I mean, uh, how are you?"

Lina was reluctant to elaborate. "I am okay, I guess. I am just trying my best to move on."

Unable to muster an apt choice of appropriate words for the moment such as this one, Rakesh stuck with an awkward 'Uh-huh'.

Lina continued, "You know, at the funeral, you gave me an envelope with a note inside with your name and phone number. Do you…"

Rakesh interrupted her again upon hearing of the note Lina referred to. "Oh Yes, I do remember very well."

The memory of the tragic event which led to the funeral of Lina's husband and daughter was still etched fresh on Rakesh's mind. Then he continued, "I am sorry, I didn't mean to be intrusive on the day I handed you the envelope. I thought…."

"No, it's alright, it's not a problem. I think you were with Mrs. Hamilton that day. Weren't you?"

"Yes, I was. She was…"

Lina didn't wait for him to complete what he wanted to say. "Uh, I don't think, uh, we've met anywhere before, I mean before the funeral, have we?"

"No, no, no… we've not," said Rakesh.

"Did you know my husband?"

"No, I never did. In fact, I must say, I don't know any of you." Rakesh was unclear about the direction of the ensuing conversation. Before Lina said anything further, Rakesh continued on. "Look, I was the one who asked Mrs. Hamilton for the details of the funeral; later we discussed few more things, one thing led to another, and I ended up accompanying her."

After a brief pause, Lina drew the conversation back to the note. "Please don't mind me asking, but don't you think it's a bit strange, even weird, to give a note, like the one you gave me, to a complete stranger?"

"Yes, I suppose. Again, I didn't mean to be intrusive and I wasn't trying to pull a scam on you or anything." There was an obvious haste and defensiveness in Rakesh's response. In a way, he was a bit taken aback, but at the same time, anticipated her question.

In a more subdued tone, Lina replied, "No, you weren't being intrusive. I wasn't sure what to make of the note. Definitely, I wasn't thinking of as a scam, well, not yet at least, since you were in the company of Mrs. Hamilton during the funeral. I must tell you, I trust her a lot. She helped me on that day and after. Anyway, I wouldn't be calling you if I thought you were scamming me."

Relieved to a certain extent by Lina's response, Rakesh proceeded further. "Well, I am glad to hear. Anyway, since you called me, I take it there is a reason?"

"I was curious, I guess," she said. Almost immediately, Lina rephrased to, "Well, maybe more than that." After a brief pause, "I've to tell you, I have received - and I still do - all sorts of mail and phone calls. A few of them were from some TV network. Every one of them has offered some sort of things, which in all honesty don't give a damn about. Then, I saw your note. Uh, yours was the only offer - if I can even use the word - which didn't ask for money. You are not asking for money, are you? Anyway, I don't think I've heard of anyone named

Rakesh. So, uh, I thought I'll give you a call and find out." There was another pause. "Coming to think of, I don't believe I even remember your face."

"That's alright. You just saw me for a brief moment at the funeral." Then he remembered someone else. "How's Madeline?"

"She's doing alright although she misses her dad and big sister, and keeps asking for them. But, I haven't figured out the best way to make her understand about what happened to them. How do you know Madeline?"

"Oh, Mrs. Hamilton told me when I spoke to her about the funeral. By the way, that's how I happened to get your name as well, in case you wondered."

In an attempt to gain further insight on Lina, Rakesh asked a different question. "By the way, do you work? I mean, are you employed someplace?"

"Yes, I am. That's been the hardest for me. My company gave me quite a chunk of time off, but I am now back to work trying to juggle between Madeline's routine and work. On top of all, I am trying to take care of all sorts of things my husband used to. That hasn't been easy at all."

"I can only imagine…." Once again, Rakesh, at a loss for the perfect selection of words, trailed off while he empathized with Lina and wondered what he should say to ease her pain.

Meanwhile, Lina persisted in her curiosity over the note. "Why did you give me the note?"

"I, uh, I don't know. I am not sure I can give you a convincing answer. I guess, I happened to notice you several times that day and I felt I should do something, if I could. That's why I attended the funeral and used the opportunity to give you the note."

"Did you mean what you wrote?"

"Of course, without a doubt." By means of an assertive and emphatic response, Rakesh hoped to allay her mix of emotions - concern, fear, suspicion, and skepticism. "Would you like to talk more about it?"

"Over the phone?"

"No, in person."

A moment of silence ensued before Lina expressed her wariness. "What's the fine print?"

"The what?"

Lina repeated her question with additional clarity. "Fine print, catch, strings. What's the catch?"

Rakesh said, "Oh, I get it. Well, there is none. Listen, you have my phone number. You can think over it and if you believe you need to discuss more, just call me. If not, we all can forget and go on with our lives. In any case, if you decide you want to talk, I'll give you one hundred percent of my attention."

There was a moment of silence during which Lina appeared to waver between thoughts. Finally she spoke. "Can we meet at a public location, uh, maybe at the library?"

"Yeah, I am fine with that," replied Rakesh. They both decided on a time, day, and the location in the library where they would meet.

After thanking Rakesh, and before hanging up the phone, Lina asked one more time, "When we meet, you won't try to sell me something, will you?"

"No, of course not."

Rakesh Jaiteley was forty years old and a bachelor. As a first generation immigrant from India, he served as a beacon of pride for his parents, for, he moved to the USA at a time when the concept of 'going to America' still evoked a sentiment of exotic novelty. Over a multitude of years, with conscientious efforts, Rakesh followed a common template adopted by many, if not all, lawful immigrants from India, and achieved the dream of settling in the United States on a permanent basis. The template encompassed a journey through numerous stages of the complex and broken US immigration system.

Eighteen years ago, at the age of twenty two, Rakesh launched his overseas adventure. After graduating with a Bachelor's degree in India, Rakesh entered the USA on a student visa as an international graduate student through an enrollment in the Master's program in Mechanical Engineering at the Cleveland Technological University, one that's not to be confused with the Cleveland Institute of Technology. The students fancifully referred themselves to as the "CeeTU'ers". The department had a total enrollment of one hundred and twelve graduate students, each at various stages of the Master's and Doctoral degree programs. Along the Department's lengthy hallway, across from the Office of the Graduate Studies, a sizeable glass-door frame hung on the wall in which lay encased the pictures and names of all the students. The pictorial of the individuals suggested, and the official records confirmed, that among the total enrolled, one hundred and three were international graduate students.

The INS – Immigration and Naturalization Service – conferred a specific designation to Rakesh by categorizing him as an F1 non-immigrant alien. The INS had since changed its popular cinematic abbreviation to the current one that was a mouthful – USCIS; the United States Citizenship and Immigration Services. The upgrade in nomenclature occurred about nine years ago, when the INS split into three different agencies under the Department of Homeland Security. USCIS was one of them. The ICE (Immigration and Customs Enforcement) and the CBP (Customs and Border Patrol) were the other two. The taxman of the USA, the IRS, awarded an official status as well for individuals such as Rakesh; he came to be known as the non-resident alien.

Within a short period of time following the kick start of the first semester, Rakesh experienced a deluge of the inevitable - homesickness, cultural shock, homework pains, and a serious dearth of money. Adding to the woes, he suffered from a lack of proper food; solely due to a conspicuous self-deficiency in cooking skills. On the positive side however, he discovered what had been lacking in his life so far – a new found independence which stemmed from the absence of his hovering parents and their incessant words of wisdom. In the end, for Rakesh, every one of these resulted in a minor degradation of his health and a major abasement of his grade point average by the time the semester culminated, for, Rakesh emerged scathed with a GPA of 3.0. Of course, an undergraduate kid might have written this off as a great achievement, but for a graduate student, anything below 3.0 meant an exile into academic probation.

Rakesh fully comprehended the implications of probation. In essence, it meant nothing but trouble, as it not only had the potential to derail one's pursuit of the academics but also could result in running afoul of the US immigration laws. In order to remain in the country and comply with the regulations, the US immigration laws required international students to maintain student status in good standing at all times.

By the second semester, Rakesh managed to clean up his act in both his academic and personal responsibilities. Regardless, over time, a traditional eighteen month stint toward graduation turned into a three year fiasco, and here was why. At the beginning of the second term, Rakesh searched for, and signed up with a professor who would act as his graduate advisor. In this capacity, the individual played a variety of roles, and one such role was to guide the student on a research topic, which at the apt moment formulated into a thesis - an essential component of the Master's program. In Rakesh's case, the professor, Dr. Walter Hantore, who had agreed to be his advisor, could not or did not identify a viable thesis topic. Rather than spending time on research, Rakesh, at the behest of Dr. Hantore, spent valuable amount of time photocopying pages of obscure journal papers. Dr. Hantore claimed that these photocopies were essential for the latest research he purported to be pursuing.

After about a year, in the midst of completing the required coursework and photocopying endless pages of seemingly meaningless research material, Rakesh learned that his advisor was slated to be terminated from the University under the charges of plagiarism. Rumor had it, a distinguished researcher from Belgium, from whom Dr. Hantore allegedly plagiarized, threatened to sue the institution. The University in turn pointed fingers at the obvious guilty fall guy - Rakesh's advisor.

Within days, Dr. Hantore disappeared and so did eighteen months of Rakesh's time in the graduate program. With both the critical aspects flushed down the drain, Rakesh embarked on a search for a new advisor with a renewed sense of urgency. He approached almost all the faculty of the department and inquired if any would be willing to take him up as their ward. During that process, Rakesh had the unfortunate pleasure of experiencing the inner politics that thrived among the higher educators. A number of faculty, many foreign born, pleasured themselves by relishing the story of the sacked professor. There was an aura of confidence that such a misfortune would never befall them and were enthralled to satisfy their bloated ego by reliving the fate of the terminated co-worker. In the midst, Rakesh became a juicy target as he was perceived guilty by association. This was shamelessly displayed by two Indian professors who, when Rakesh approached them, took great pleasure in ridiculing Rakesh about his ex-advisor. Apparently, these top-notch educated PhDs determined that harassing a foreign graduate student and fellow countryman was a brilliant venture to pursue within the academia.

In the end, one of them, Dr. Mindy Bates, accepted Rakesh as her ward. Dr. Bates was a fresh PhD graduate and a brand new faculty in the department. She was in desperate need for graduate students, research topics, and research money in order to churn out papers and secure her tenure while Rakesh was in desperate need of an advisor. The symbiosis worked like a charm. Besides, Dr. Bates turned out to be the most amicable person Rakesh had ever met. She kept up a jovial personality and all the students loved her attitude and temperament. Sometimes, Rakesh wondered if Dr. Bates would have been a better fit at the Disney World rather than in academia. Much to Rakesh's relief, Dr. Bates also demonstrated a high level of competence, which translated into her ability to concoct a thesis topic robust enough to muster support from the thesis committee, which was made up of three faculty members. With copious efforts, Rakesh ensured that the two

Indian professors remained anywhere but in his thesis committee.

By summer of the third year in the program, the prospect of graduation became stronger and Rakesh embarked on a search for a full time job. This process turned out to be the next step of the journey for foreign students aspiring to settle in the United States forever.

With meticulous planning, Rakesh formulated a path which encompassed ascertaining minimal to zero lapse in time between his graduation and the start of a new job. Two factors fed the necessary impetus for this extent of planning – continued state of poor finances and the requirement to maintain lawful status in the USA. Of course, these were easier said than done. At the time, the country suffered from a notable recession; as a result, employers deployed an overt practice of hierarchical preference on who they would hire for the scant number of open positions. Those with numerous years of experience, who were also in all likelihood high wage earners, faced the brunt of layoff under the euphemism of 'redundancy elimination'. The same individuals now became highly preferred by other employers, as these folks were desperate enough to accept lower wage jobs, which turned out to be what the employers aimed for in the first place. Within this vicious cycle of employment circle, graduating students with zero experience had almost no chance of securing a full time career. The plight of the international students was further more dismal. This narrow group of aspiring employees required employer sponsorship for a work visa – something that came with a high cost and significant time delay for the employers. Consequently, Rakesh and his kind fell beneath the bottom of the desired candidate pool.

Meanwhile, for Rakesh, the graduation event arrived and ended with no sign of a job. Since his F1 status held its validity only for the duration of the studies, it signaled an obvious end of his legal stay in the USA. To avoid the risk of losing legal status, the University's Director of the International Student Office, Mr. Parker Wu a veteran himself in the journey to the USA - encouraged Rakesh and other foreign victims of US recession to enroll in another lateral or advance level graduate program. This, Mr. Wu reasoned, would allow the students to extend their F1 status. Rakesh did just that by enrolling in another Master's program with a different area of specialization. This time around, he was canny enough to choose Dr. Bates as his advisor right from day one.

As the fresh pursuit began, the planets and the stars aligned in favor of Rakesh, at least on the money front. The assistantship package that Rakesh received provided him with a monthly stipend of a little over two thousand dollars in addition to the one hundred percent paid tuition. While the research grant paid him a little over eight hundred dollars a month, the remainder of the money materialized through Dr. Bates' effective manipulation of the University's assistantship policy loopholes. This fantastic loophole allowed Rakesh to earn the additional monies by teaching an undergraduate class and grading homework for other faculty members. With less than six hundred dollars of monthly expense, something that was feasible as a result of an ultra frugal lifestyle followed by most foreign Asian students, Rakesh's income to expense ratio was fabulous. He felt rich and, over time, became comfortable with the way of life.

Another three years flew by at Cleveland Technological University. By now, Rakesh became an established veteran CeeTU'er. However, also by now, everything seemed to get on his nerves. The city bored him and his one room efficiency apartment felt like a cage. Truth and fiction about foreign students finding lucrative jobs in other cities made him irritable. Several batches of new Indian students, fresh from the land he left a few years ago, did not impress him in any means positive, as a fair number of them prospered in their pursuit of education by means of copying others' homework and projects. With a load of scornful, but influencing reasons, Rakesh rushed to complete his thesis; he decided to get out of the University, once and for all.

With his mind made up, Rakesh migrated to the next step of the immigration journey. He applied for the Optional Practical Training (OPT) with the INS. The OPT, a provision of the immigration law, conferred employment authorization to an F1 holder after completion of studies. Multiple variants existed in the law's provision; however, in its simplest make up, OPT, at that time allowed legal employment for a maximum of one year by letting the applicant accept any job as long as it related to the applicant's field of study. For most foreign students however, the OPT became the Almighty's endearing gift since it served as a convenient bridge to transition from an F1 student to an H1 full time worker.

In addition, the OPT allowed the international student to remain in the US after graduation, even if the student did not possess an employment offer. This provision blessed the job seekers with precious time within which one could search and secure employment. Of course, the students had to play it safe and determine if the OPT was in their best interest since, in a recession, it could lead to the OPT permit lapsing without any jobs in sight. If that occurred, it would result in a disastrous waste of a golden provision allowed by the INS. Another benefit of the OPT lay in the fact that the foreigner could begin full time work and remain employed while the employer and the employee waited for the work visa sponsorship application to be adjudicated by the INS.

The loosely termed 'work visa' was nothing but the H1 status that allowed foreigners to be employed in the US upon satisfying INS' various criteria. As it remained the case in numerous INS provisions, the H1 carried multiple designations, each specific to certain categories of foreign individuals. The law required the employer to petition an individual for the H1 status and pay the required fee. In other words, a foreigner could not sponsor him or herself to become an H1 holder. For the foreign employee, this signified a state of complete dependence on a specific employer and any change in employer or employment mandated a filing of a new petition. That extent of dependence was not a major issue when employed with a reputable firm. However, there also existed a number of outfits - notoriously prevalent within the IT industry - that titled themselves as 'consultants'. These shady consultants flouted as many immigration laws as they could muster while taking extreme precautions to stay one step ahead from being caught. They used fake job postings and fake resumes as a means to obtain H1B approvals. Once the foreign workers entered the roster, the 'consultants' openly exploited them, knowing well, the worker with questionable qualifications would rather endure the exploitation than squeal. After all, what kind of employee would risk losing the opportunity to achieve the American dream? One common mode of abuse among these 'consultants' was the failure to pay the prevailing wages stipulated in the H1B petition. The other form entailed payment of the agreed wages in order to maintain a clean payroll record; however, they later forced the employee to refund a portion of the salary in cash.

By the time Rakesh graduated with the second Master's and held a successful Optional Practical Training work permit in hand, the US economy began prospering and consumers started consuming. Fresh graduates in the west coast of the country called themselves entrepreneurs and started anything and everything as long as their venture ended with a '.com'. For a majority of them however, the dot-com ending of their startups would also spell the end of their startup altogether. Despite the outcome, many did become instant millionaires with cold hard cash. In the meantime, many others who became millionaires on paper discovered the paper to be worthless upon the demise of their venture.

In the Midwest, the auto industry was no exception. The US auto sales sustained at a steady number between sixteen and seventeen million vehicles, a number considered healthy by most analysts. Career opportunities flourished, even for fresh graduates, especially in the metropolitan Detroit area. In a natural transition of things, sometime in the fall that year, Rakesh found his first job as an entry level engineer at an automotive component manufacturer in the Detroit suburb of Sterling Heights. The human resources group, familiar with the work visa sponsorship process, filed a successful and non-frivolous petition on behalf of Rakesh Jaiteley. Within four months, INS approved the petition and distinguished Rakesh as an H1B non-immigrant alien. The IRS, on the other hand, defined H1B foreigners as resident aliens. For Rakesh, this meant two major differences. One, he'd have to use form 1040 - meant for residents - instead of the 1040NR, which was relegated to non-residents and F1 students. Second, Social Security taxes would now be withheld from his paycheck, something he escaped while as a student.

With H1B in hand, Rakesh planted the seeds for his next step of his settlement journey. He approached the company's human resources to discuss the possibility of a green card sponsorship. If he succeeded in obtaining the green card, he would become a lawful permanent resident of the US, thereby allowing him to live and work without major restrictions. Similar to the H1, it was the employer who had to sponsor the employment-based green card; therefore, the entire process danced to the whims of the employer. The HR, after much discussion, agreed to commence the process as soon as Rakesh completed six more months of employment with the company. Where or how HR got this pre-condition was unknown; nevertheless, Rakesh couldn't do much as he was at the mercy of the employer for his green card, and would remain so for the next several years.

In the meantime, Rakesh settled into a one-bedroom apartment in the city of Beniton Heights. Among the number of Detroit suburbs, Beniton Heights ranked as the top five on a multitude of categories. The everyday commute however, was nothing to be boastful about, for, it consumed more than an hour each way for a mere twenty-five miles. The nineteen mile stretch of the east-west interstate 696, which Rakesh normally took, was notorious for its congestion and therefore took the lion's share of the commuting time.

Six months later, in the middle of the following year, as agreed upon, the company began Rakesh's application for a green card. The process, riddled with its own ridiculous levels of complexity, involved multiple steps, and in all certainty, several years. In the first step, a Labor Certification was filed, in which the company had to prove it could not identify a qualified US citizen or permanent resident for the position.

The submission of such a proof snaked through several layers of processes, one of which included efforts to recruit other potential qualified candidates. In a way, a carefully choreographed act between a qualified attorney and the employer ensured a successful Labor Certification application. In other words, a highly competent immigration attorney and a well-organized job duties, roles, and responsibilities helped vouch for the sponsored applicant by asserting the applicant to be the best, thereby disqualifying all others. During Rakesh's era, the process of Labor Certification approval took a few years.

The second stage involved filing the immigrant petition using the I-140 form. Not surprisingly, the I-140 also took its time to work its way through the approval process. The third and final step entailed the filing of the form I-485. This step came to be known as the Adjustment of Status, in which the applicant, upon the form's approval, switched from the status of a non-immigrant to a permanent resident. However, there existed a catch – a big one. The United States admitted only a certain number of permanent residents per year from each country. The applicants' country of birth, therefore, determined and drove the adjustment stage of the process. In addition, the I-485 could only be filed if immigrant visa numbers were available or, put another way, only if the numerical maximum was not reached. The visa availability was determined based on the date the governing agency received the initial Labor Certification. This date came to be known as the priority date. Unfortunately, due to the high demand from applicants born in certain countries - India, China, Mexico and the Philippines, to be specific – and because of the limited number of immigrant visas available per year, painful levels of backlogs occurred and grew. Someone such as Rakesh, who was born in India, therefore had to wait until the priority date became current and a visa number materialized, prior to filing the I-485. This resulted in an agonizing wait for several years.

In addition to the waiting time, other restrictions existed as well. For one, the law, for the most part, deprived the sponsored individual from accepting any new positions within the same employer or another one. Doing so carried the potential of jeopardizing the entire green card process. This restriction limited one's ability to move up the career ladder or transition to another employer. Over the years, as INS morphed into USCIS and migrated under the umbrella of the Department of Homeland Security, several immigration laws were enacted, changed and deleted, few of which barely benefited the green card applicants who waited an endless number of years. The public considered immigration and immigrants to be synonymous with the unknown millions of undocumented aliens living illegally in the USA. The politicians and the media nurtured and encouraged such a view. In the end, people applying for lawful permanent residence had a very minimal number of laws and provisions in their favor. So the wait for the elusive green card continued.

Four years later, the USCIS approved the I-140 immigrant petition. With the visa numbers still not available, Rakesh's employer remained unable to file the final Adjustment of Status application. Since no one had the capacity to predict the availability of the visa, Rakesh decided it was in his best interest not to hold up his life decisions and aspirations any longer under the pretext of waiting for the green card.

In his pursuit of the American dream, Rakesh purchased and moved into a condo in the same suburb of Beniton Heights, where he lived now. He reasoned he was better off not draining his money on rent; rather build equity on the property while availing favorable tax deductions available to homeowners. Rakesh chose a skinny, three floors high, eighteen hundred square feet, three-bedroom condo unit whose street level contained the 'basement' and a one-car garage. The center section, the level one, hosted the kitchen and the family room, along with a half bath. Level two held the three bedrooms and two full baths. Beniton Heights, among other things, prided itself for being a top ranking public-school district, which translated into a strong potential for higher property values.

In the meantime, as Rakesh patiently waited month after month for some signs – any signs - of visa number availability, his career stagnated or showed meager growth. He had to endure it all in the name of protecting his green card process and preventing it from derailing. Rakesh's Manager, however, recognizing his well above-average performance empathized with him on the arduous permanent residency process and was gracious enough to pull as many strings within his means to ensure Rakesh received decent salary increases every year. In addition, if the HR's bureaucracy and the immigration rules allowed, his Manager grabbed the opportunity to confer Rakesh innovative job titles in an attempt to match his ever increasing work experience.

At last, one summer, eight years after he started his employment at his current company, the USCIS approved the I-485 Adjustment of Status application. Rakesh Jaiteley became a lawful permanent resident of the United States. The USCIS mailed him a Notice of Action - Form I-797. On the message section of the notice, the title read, 'Welcome to the United States of America'. The second sentence of the notice's first paragraph said, 'It is with great pleasure that we welcome you to permanent resident status in the United States.' By then, Rakesh had lived in the USA for almost fourteen years. The absurdity of the title on the notice made him chuckle out loud.

With the green card in hand, next came the euphoria of freedom – the freedom from being tied to a certain employer or a certain job; the freedom from the constant worry of renewing his H1 petition; and the freedom from the stress of applying for the US visa which required a pilgrimage to a US consulate outside the United States. As a first step toward capitalizing on this freedom, Rakesh wasted no time in seeking a new career.

The USA was by now again in a recession. The economists and other pundits coined an official term - the 'Great Recession'. However, in this round, Rakesh sensed he had an upper hand on multiple fronts. He held an advanced degree from a reputable US University - in fact two advanced degrees, not that two made any tangible difference. In addition, he had several years of valuable work experience. But the most important of all was the fact that Rakesh had the ability to accept employment anywhere in the US without requiring any work visa sponsorship.

In November of that year, Rakesh began his new career. It was with Milamek Corporation, a publicly traded, global engineering and manufacturing company. As a senior level Manager in Engineering, he commanded a lucrative salary plus few perks. The new role resulted in a major and positive departure from his previous job, both in terms of compensation and authority. Despite mass layoffs - commonplace during that year – Rakesh's position became available as a by-product of an acquisition which Milamek Corporation had completed in the recent past. The acquired company, a private enterprise in Rochester Hills - another prime suburb of Detroit - was renamed into a new Division of Milamek Corporation.

Milamek had a standard procedure after every acquisition and it was called the 'Business Integration'. In plain terms, the company deployed what it called the 'Integration Team' to the new facility with the sole goal of bringing everything and everyone in line with Milamek's standardized global policies and systems. As an added bonus, this also presented an opportunity for Milamek Corporation to eliminate head count redundancies at the acquired firm. As a result, besides whatever integration it did, there was an organized and structured termination of employees. The first set of casualties almost always happened to be the top two to three layers of the management. Next in line on the butcher's block were the dissenters, naysayers, and the ubiquitous stubborn who hated change and were hell bent on resisting anything and everything which fell in their path.

Interestingly enough, by now, the cleaning of the house triggered an acute shortfall in the head count, for a significant chunk of the terminations stemmed out of politics than necessity. The shortfall was then compensated by means of the company advertising them as new opportunities which were then, in part, taken up by existing personnel from other Divisions of Milamek and, in part, by fresh blood from the outside. Rakesh Jaiteley ended up as one of the fresh blood outsiders. His new daily commute worsened to thirty five miles each way; however, most of it remained on freeways. If there was a bright spot in his commute, it was the fact that it took the same amount of commuting time as it did at the last place of work. In any event, he still had to meander his way through interstate 696, which persisted in its notorious congestion during peak hours, despite high levels of unemployment in the region at the time.

Rakesh was by then thirty six years old and still a bachelor, much to the dismay of his aging parents who lived in India. Rakesh's parents never once ended their phone calls without reminding him of his pariah bachelor status. There were plenty of girls vying to marry him, his parents stressed, and his mom persistently sent pictures and biographies of these supposedly desperate and vying girls. His parents even hoped, against their beliefs, that Rakesh might have a secret girlfriend – had to be an Indian, of course – someone worthy to be married to their son. Rakesh, for his part, denied any existence of girlfriends – secretive or otherwise - and refused to consider marriage.

In the meantime, Rakesh grew accustomed to his laid back, yet an enjoyable and comfortable bachelor lifestyle. He couldn't imagine himself as a family guy with a wife and a couple of kids in tow; he cherished his current way of living where he did whatever pleased him, most of which were mundane anyway. During weekdays, he engaged himself in eventful work days, played tennis with his friends for a couple of evenings, watched TV, buried his thoughts in a few online forums debating the world issues in anonymity, and went to a movie or two in the theaters once in a while. This routine had him occupied and busy until bedtime. During weekends, his life became dreadfully comparable to any normal family guy with chores ranging from laundry to grocery shopping. However, the most he enjoyed on Saturdays and Sundays was the sleep-in which extended almost through the morning hours.

By now, Rakesh had been employed at Milamek Corporation for

almost four years. The pace of his lifestyle in those years had evolved as well, along with his age as he recently turned forty. His work kept him extremely occupied and the significant chunk of the current year seemed to have flown by fast as it was already the middle of October. Rakesh yearned for the holiday mood that usually pervaded the entire workforce just before Thanksgiving in late November and continued through the first week of the New Year. He looked forward for the slowdown in the pace of work that accompanied the holiday spirits.

~~~   3   ~~~

The school district in the city of Beniton Heights controlled the administration and the operation of nine elementary, six middle, and four high schools. Despite the rising property values, Beniton Heights continued to experience a growing influx of families with young children – testament to the enviably high ranking of the school district. As far as elementary schools, among all, Hadley Lyons Elementary ranked the highest. As a result, a relatively higher demand for enrollment persisted at this institution, not to mention the demand for housing which lay within the jurisdiction of Hadley Lyons.

Karen Wharton served as one of six kindergarten teachers at the Hadley Lyons Elementary School.

The school housed up to the fifth grade with a total enrollment hovering close to six hundred. According to the school's website, the most recent head count stood at five hundred and ninety three with an average student-teacher ratio of 17.5. Every grade at Hadley Lyons had at least six sections while a couple of them carried more. The kindergarten class had one hundred and fourteen children with an equal number per section. Karen's class of nineteen children represented the vast diversity of Beniton Heights' demographics, and in general, the diversity of the metro Detroit region itself.

The access to the elementary school began on Shaver Road which intersected with the busy Macomb Line Road. The hustle and bustle of traffic on Macomb Line vanished instantly as soon as one made a turn into Shaver. A few hundred feet into Shaver, a number of single family ranches and colonials presented themselves on either side of the street which wound along a gentle hill all the way to the top. The sidewalks along both sides of the road and the yards of the homes demonstrated caring qualities of the residents and the city alike. The backyards of few of the homes on the north side of Shaver Road backed into the school grounds. Residents of these homes had a pleasing view of the children playing on the school property. These houses, built more than a couple of decades ago, proved the maturity of the neighborhood by virtue of the well grown trees – sugar maple, red maple, crabapple, weeping willow, and the black spruce, to name a few – on the properties.

At the top of the hill, Shaver Road curved to the left, becoming Lyons Avenue for the remaining three hundred feet or so before ending at the sprawling grounds of the school property. The school itself was built and opened in the nineties to meet the demand of the growing young family population. Since then, there had been renovations and upgrades in order to conform to the newer codes, technology, and ever growing safety and security requirements. The residents of the road leading to the school coped with the constant presence of the building contractors every summer when building work spiked.

Karen Wharton had been a public school teacher for over ten years and had been teaching the kindergarten class at Hadley Lyons Elementary for a little over six years. While the media indulged in sensationalizing anything they perceived to be good for their business - such as reports of incompetent teachers or teachers in inappropriate relationships with their students - the reality at Hadley Lyons Elementary, and for that matter, the school district itself, remained far from that. These teachers were outstanding. The educators overcame the constraints of the politics of the public educational system, and went above and beyond to ensure academic excellence for their wards.

Karen Wharton was no exception. As a matter of fact, the former school where she taught considered her departure a tangible loss for the school. One of her highly commendable qualities was her willingness and diligence in undertaking the efforts to identify the competency levels of the students in her class well at the beginning of the academic year. She then improvised and fine-tuned the curriculum to the standards that would meet the requirements of the children to the best possible extent. In the past several years, she discerned an increased level of competency among the students entering her kindergarten class. This in part, appeared to be due to parents' involvement, and as well an ever evolving diversity in demographics. Based on such observations, Karen continually strengthened her teaching material, and as a means to aid her efforts, she deployed the practice of maintaining diligent notes of every student's strengths, weaknesses, and performance trends. By the time summer rolled in at the end of the academic year, Karen's kindergarteners became competent enough to get through the first grade with minimal efforts.

At the time Karen accepted the teaching position at Hadley Lyons

Elementary, she was fully aware of the positive reputation of the school district and this particular school. Consequently, she aspired to have her twin boys, Jake and Josh, who at that time were four years old, to attend Hadley Lyons Elementary. It was therefore, an easy decision for her family to find housing in Beniton Heights within the jurisdiction of Hadley Lyons. Soon after relocating to the city, the twins had enough time to settle before they commenced kindergarten the following academic year.

Both Karen Wharton and the twins were excited at the fact that they would all be together at the same school. Once Karen began her new teaching assignment, she made arrangements to have her twins in her class. The twins, needless to say, were ecstatic to have their mother as their teacher as well. Besides the fun factor, for Karen and family, it turned out to be a very practical approach, allowing the twins to remain in the in-school child care until Karen wrapped up her day's work.

That was five years ago. Now, it was the middle of October and the two boys were grown up and attending fifth grade. Karen and her husband looked forward to the Thanksgiving break less than a month away followed by the Christmas break. The twins however, had an agenda of their own and were gearing up for Halloween about a couple of weeks away.

The next several weeks, leading to the end of year holiday, were expected to be hectic for the teachers at Hadley Lyons Elementary. Multiple deadlines loomed and a number of reports and actions needed to be completed. The first of which happened to be during the week of Halloween, when the school operated on a half-day schedule on three days - Monday, Wednesday and Friday. The half days on Monday and Friday were planned for the parent-teacher meetings which usually extended well into late evening. The half day on Wednesday the October 31st - which also happened to be the day the children observed Halloween - was planned to accommodate the faculty development meeting. The scheduling also allowed children to leave school earlier in order to prepare for an exciting Halloween night. Karen had emailed the sign-up sheet and the schedule for the parent-teacher meeting to the parents few weeks ago; consequently, she had by now received most of the sign-ups from the kindergarteners' parents and guardians. There were still some open slots and inevitably few last minute stragglers, and Karen waited for those to be filled up soon.

~~~   4   ~~~

Rakesh Jaiteley lived a contrasting personal and career lifestyle. Outside of work, he maintained, and enjoyed a calm and mundane schedule – mostly by containing all forms of responsibilities to an absolute bare minimum. At his job, the opposite prevailed. By no means was he a workaholic; however, he refused to remain content on just getting by performing his slated job duties. In the four years he had been with Milamek Corporation, Rakesh fostered an enviable level of professional relationship with personnel across the entire hierarchy of the Division's organization. He exuded a down-to-earth persona with a willingness to plunge in, take the necessary initiative, and get the task completed. Rakesh maintained a strong work ethic and treated his direct reports in a fair manner while also setting an expectation of above-average performance and a sense of self-accountability. Rakesh despised repetitive tasks; therefore, actively solicited new assignments, projects and training, even if they happened to be from other departments or groups. With an innate ability to maintain composure amid contentious discussion – which seemed all too common in any organization with numerous personalities – Rakesh, with minimal effort, maneuvered difficult situations that required urgent solutions without attracting undesirable emotions. As a result of his positive personality traits and superior technical skills, Rakesh commanded a laudable reputation among his superiors, peers and sub-ordinates alike.

During his first year at Milamek Corporation, in the midst of a critical project, Rakesh discovered a serious, but a well-known, deficiency wherein the new development projects were not being tracked, archived or managed in an effective manner. This failed to aid the cross-functional teams as it resulted in their inability to extract meaningful information. Milamek, at its corporate level, had a standardized system. Due to the recent nature of the acquisition, Rakesh's Division had not yet integrated with that system. Besides, the integration of the corporate level systems had so far been anything but seamless. In any event, the various teams, including Rakesh's, bore the brunt of the system's deficiency.

In the end, Rakesh took the initiative to find a solution to mitigate the sense of chaos. He developed a package utilizing tools familiar to him from a long number of years ago. The package was rudimentary but robust enough to serve the team's purpose. When Rakesh rolled it out to his Division, the department heads loved it and embraced it in an instant. It took two years before Milamek's corporate system was fully integrated into Rakesh's Division and another full year before the Division completely abandoned his package in favor of the mandated corporate system.

Regardless, Rakesh's similar initiatives on multiple fronts - especially as a freshman employee - received the attention, and even a bit of envy of John Wharton. John, one of a dozen or so Project Managers in the Division, held the job responsibility which required an intricate involvement in the project activities owned by other teams. John had been with this Division of Milamek Corporation for about six months before Rakesh came on board. Prior to that, John was stationed at another campus of Milamek Corporation, also in Rochester Hills three miles from the new Division. Abundant rumors floated among the workforce which suggested Milamek might consolidate the two campuses – with potential loss of jobs. So far, the rumors remained just that, and everyone went on with their lives.

John Wharton and his family had relocated to the metro Detroit area from Morehead, Kentucky where Milamek Corporation operated a manufacturing plant. Morehead, with a population of around seven thousand was located along interstate 64 and US highway 60. Milamek Corporation, like many others in the USA, in the interest of maintaining lower labor cost, established manufacturing plants in smaller cities and towns. Morehead happened to be one of the small city lucky winners of blue collar jobs. Many global corporations perceived such smaller locations as both a benefit and a drawback. On one hand, it was a challenge to find and recruit the necessary talent since many preferred large metropolitan areas as diverse employment options existed without the need to relocate too far. On the other hand, many called these small communities home; therefore, possessed an inclination to remain with an employer long term. This was partly due to the limited employment options available elsewhere within the city. In the former scenario, the employers had to attract individuals with higher compensation. In the latter, the employers got away paying stagnant and low wages. Either way, if locations such as Morehead impacted the corporations' profit targets, the companies moved to border towns in Mexico or in more recent times, to China and other lower cost countries. At the end of it all, the effects of the volatility and offshoring were pretty obvious - the CEO's and the executives continued to rake their millions while the white collar employees with technical background, experience, and education sustained and survived through voluntary and involuntary relocation. The hourly blue-collar workers in the meantime, suffered the most impact, and endured the ill effects of long-term unemployment.

John Wharton was married to Karen Wharton, the kindergarten teacher at Hadley Lyons Elementary. Karen taught at a public school in Morehead before their relocation to Beniton Heights. Despite the fact John enjoyed his tenure at Milamek Corporation, both he and Karen aspired to relocate to a larger metropolitan area. They sought wider options for education, shopping, housing, social life and demographic diversity. The schools, specifically, floated high in their minds as their twins Jake and Josh were slated to begin kindergarten in a little more than a year. As he explored numerous options, John was offered the opportunity to relocate his work base to the Rochester Hills campus of Milamek Corporation. Karen also sought a public school teaching position in the Detroit area. After an aggressive search, she landed her current role as the kindergarten teacher at Hadley Lyons Elementary. This fortunate sequence of events allowed the family to relocate to Beniton Heights about six years ago.

John's envy of Rakesh was fortunately friendly and competitive in nature. With an equally assertive and motivated personality who believed in working smart, John became increasingly inquisitive to learn more about his new co-worker. Consequently, John cultivated a habit, as long as time permitted, to stop by Rakesh's office and discuss challenging subject matter of mutual interest. John quizzed Rakesh on a variety of projects as a means to learn something new, and if any piqued his attention, John volunteered to be a part of the project - as long as John's Manager and the rest of the office politics were agreeable. This motivated spirit helped John learn a variety of applications and put an equal number of them to beneficial practical use. For some strange reason, John felt compelled to compete despite the fact Rakesh did not consider himself as special in any way. Over time, this friendly competition between the two men evolved into a close personal friendship.

Soon after that, John introduced Rakesh to his wife, Karen Wharton, and the twins, Jake and Josh. In what seemed a natural progression of their friendship, John invited his bachelor co-worker to his home on a frequent basis. On a number of occasions, Rakesh had dinner at the Whartons and spent several hours of conversational time with John and Karen well after the kids went to bed. As time passed, Rakesh slowly, but at a steady pace, learned the art of dealing with the two kids and soon enough became an expert in entertaining the twins with all sorts of silly games.

The ever growing friendship between Rakesh and John's family had a positive side effect on Rakesh. With the exception of the sleeping-in on weekends, Rakesh became a lot more active in his personal life. This was in part due to his involvement in John's seemingly never ending do-it-yourself projects, for, John excelled as a dexterous handyman. He called on Rakesh anytime he needed an extra pair of hands for his pet projects in and around his home. In the beginning, Rakesh displayed an extraordinary level of clumsiness while handling the tools and materials, but over a period of time, he managed to display a bit of improvement. With Rakesh's turn to envy John, he propelled himself, with a solid determination, to learn few basic home repairs from John.

If there was one thing Rakesh failed to account for in his elaborate calculation of home ownership costs, it happened to be the cost of hiring someone to handle any repairs. Rakesh's gross inability to fix something even simple unraveled as rapidly as the arrival of the first mortgage statement. A short time after moving in, the water in the toilet ran and he hired a plumber who in turn replaced the rubber flush valve and charged Rakesh a hefty one hundred and six dollars and thirty seven cents for 'parts and labor'. The plumber spent less than ten minutes and made easy money that day while Rakesh skipped few heart beats for having to shell out that kind of money.

Over the years, Rakesh managed to accumulate a decent arsenal of tools, more out of fascination while wandering the aisles of the mega home improvement stores. In the meantime, most of what he bought remained with nothing more than scant use. However, he also learned a few 'do-it-yourself' tricks in a solid determination to cut down the handyman bills to the bare minimum. In any event, he was no match for John Wharton. In the past several years of home ownership, John had completed an impressive array of projects which Rakesh could only dream.

By now, Rakesh's friendship with the Wharton family grew to be a close one. Rakesh observed with amazement how busy the Whartons were. He compared to his lowly bachelor life which, if not for John's projects and alliance, remained far less hectic. Rakesh eventually dared to venture beyond his comfort level by offering to watch the twins and take them to the mall or the movies. He felt Karen and John could use some lone moment to themselves which seemed to be a rarity for the couple. The twins were always excited to spend time with 'Mr. Rakesh' since they knew they could get away with almost anything. For Rakesh however, those events were exhausting as he had to keep up and learn new parenting skills; something he lacked. In addition, he had to be acutely beware of every trick and manipulation the twins deployed at him. In any case, he enjoyed the experience and further to it, he enjoyed his friendship with the Wharton family.

Yet another positive outcome of the friendship with the Wharton family turned out to be the fabulous food that Rakesh enjoyed, for, Karen was a great cook. Every time Rakesh went to the Whartons for dinner - which these days seemed to be almost two or three times a week - Karen made it a point to prepare a sumptuous dinner. Rakesh, a non-picky eater, showed a willingness to try different items. His favorites however, were the meat loaf, mashed potatoes, and the salad with bits of apple and cranberries tossed in them. He savored the freshness of the food prepared from scratch, considering the fact that Rakesh's diet was anything as long as they emerged from his freezer.

Rakesh's cooking - if that was indeed the right word - was designed for survival and not for enjoyment. Once about every two to three weeks, Rakesh paid a visit to the Badsha Asian Groceries or BAGS as it was more popularly known among the Indians. The store, located about two miles east of Rakesh's condo on Chatham Street off Maple Road, carried an impressive inventory of aromatic Indian and Pakistani groceries that included instant food mixes, frozen curries, fresh produce, spices, lentils and Indian snacks. Rakesh's shopping list tilted heavily in favor of frozen and processed food, all of them laden with levels of spiciness nothing lower than medium-hot. The result was rather evident his refrigerator had its freezer stuffed to the brim while the rest of the unit remained quite bare. Rakesh did manage to stock up on milk, juice, bread, and jelly in addition to an assortment of blazing hot Indian pickles.

As with most employees at Milamek, this year had so far been quite hectic for John Wharton. Even as the middle of October rolled in, his busy schedule showed no signs of abating. Lately, John's work load only increased; something attributable to the improved employment market. In the past few months, an unusual number of employees left Milamek Corporation to 'pursue other interests'. As it always seemed to be the case, the process of hiring replacements moved at a snail's pace as the recruitment 'paperwork' meandered through an untold number of mandatory steps within the human resources bureaucracy. Therefore, besides handling his own projects, John had to take on a few other projects that were managed before by another individual. In addition, he had to travel to other sites in and outside of the US. Even as the year wound down with end of October less than a couple of weeks away, John had a few more trips lined up, all the way until the Christmas break. Anytime John traveled out of town, Rakesh offered to help out with anything within his means if Karen so wished. Karen most certainly appreciated the support.

~~~   5   ~~~

In early July – a little over three months ago, the summer was bright and hot, and so was Arnie Casper's outlook of the future, for, he at last received the long awaited exhilarating information. He experienced a palpable sense of relief and he had good reasons. After sporadic and desperate employment stints for the past more than three years, a full time opportunity, beginning the following month, beckoned him.

Arnie always considered himself to be dedicated and a hard working individual; however, the economy and his ex-employers had been indifferent to his self-evaluation - maybe even indiscriminate.

Until April, three and a half years ago, Arnie worked at a six-hundred employee auto parts manufacturing enterprise in metro Detroit. He had been in loyal service with this firm for over two decades. Seven months prior to April, the winds of change crept in. The privately owned company made a hurried announcement and began the first round of layoffs. The company just reacted to the ongoing downturn in its business and the country's economy in general. The layoff affected fourteen employees scattered across multiple departments. Arnie Casper worked as an hourly employee in the Facilities and Maintenance department whose responsibilities included building maintenance, housekeeping, mail-sorting, and security. He worked the day shift and managed to survive this layoff.

Three months following the first round, sometime in January, the company made a dire announcement of sharp downturn in sales, not to mention the negative forecast for the next several months. An email memo went around in which the employees were told to brace for an imminent and a significant layoff which would entail a reduction in workforce by at least fifteen percent. This impending execution notice turned out to be far less tolerable than the surprise layoff which occurred three months ago. No one knew when the actual terminations would occur or who might be impacted.

One day, on a Tuesday morning in mid-February, ninety-four employees received the pink slip. The company asserted that the elimination involved only the redundant and non-essential positions – "trimming the fat" as it was referred to in casual speak. The majority of the casualties in this round were employees who had devoted their lives to the company – a number of administrative assistants, several layers of Managers and more than sixty hourly employees. Arnie and few other hourly employees resented the ugly fact that there were a disproportionate number of hourly employees among the eliminated group. It vindicated their suspicion that the lopsided impact on the hourly employees was solely due to lack of protection and representation by a Union. To make matters worse, the company transferred Arnie to the night shift.

Regrettably for the employees, the layoffs did not cease in February. There were to be few more rounds. The next round occurred at the end of the month, and then two more, one each in the next couple of months. During each of these layoffs, the hourly workers bore the biggest brunt in terms of the number of people. The total casualty stood at little over two hundred.

Arnie was terminated from his employment in April.

By this time, tens of thousands of workers across the United States, with varying skill levels and pent up anxiety, sought new employment, while the economy, in deep recession, made it impossible to find one within a short period of time.

Arnie Casper endured a depressing struggle for the next three years in an attempt to return to a full time job that doled out a steady paycheck. Instead, at best, he received only short term offers. These were hourly contracts in building maintenance and security. Needless to say, these brief assignments carried no benefits. On top of that, once the contract ended, Arnie returned to seek the next opportunity, resulting in long bouts of unemployment in between, which was excruciating at best. At one point, Arnie tried his hands at one of the major home hardware retailers. Too bad for Arnie, the stores were trending to the future, which in this case entailed the installation of numerous self-service checkout lanes. Consequently, a number of employees suffered termination according to their seniority, and Arnie happened to be one of the first few to be released from employment. He then substituted as a parking lot security guard anytime a regular employee was off or did not care to show up. This forced Arnie to work unpredictable shifts and hours with no sense of regularity and of course, zero benefits.

In short, Arnie realized he did not have too many options in the career market. For one, Arnie's educational credentials boasted of a high school diploma which served as nothing more than a monstrous barrier to a successful full time employment. Arnie's education or lack thereof turned out to be a very convenient excuse for employers as they received hundreds, if not thousands, of resumes for every available position.

Arnie recognized his handicap and decided to shift directions. He made few serious attempts to improve his marketability. Based on his past experience in the areas of building maintenance and security, Arnie enrolled and completed a couple of facilities certification courses, including HVAC and Electrical training courses. He also took a defensive firearms course. Arnie hoped, somehow these courses would make his résumé furthermore attractive. On the flip side, completing a multitude of courses also meant a significant drain of money and there was only so much Arnie could spend on these expensive courses. Moreover, he remained clueless on the tangible benefit these certifications might provide in terms of securing a full time position.

Two years after he lost his job at the auto parts company, Arnie caught the much needed break. He was thrilled when he received an offer for a full time position at a local manufacturing plant. All the more exciting - a well-known regional Union represented the hourly work force, something Arnie had been yearning. Arnie trusted this job to be the one which would support his livelihood for the foreseeable long term. However, he also learned that the Management and the Union had recently negotiated a new contract that allowed the deployment of a two-tier wage structure for the Union employees. In other words, anyone who had been employed preceding the signing of the new contract would be paid a starting wage of $18 an hour for the same position Arnie was hired in. Those hired under the terms of the new contract would earn a starting wage of only $11 an hour. In addition, the probationary period for the Union employees was increased from three months to six. Any employee on probation could be terminated at will with no further support from the Union, and without any possibility of appeal.

Arnie weighed in the options – he could accept a full time position at second tier wage or remain unemployed for an unpredictable amount of time. He chose the former. Soon after he began his gig at the manufacturing firm, Arnie witnessed something he did not expect – a callous and a contemptuous sense of work ethic among the longer tenured, higher paid Union employees; employees who were hired prior to the current contract. Besides, the higher paid employees had the security of due process in the event of an impending layoff – something Arnie lacked, at least until the end of the probationary period. Arnie, as a result, found himself working disproportionately harder than his higher waged counterparts; a discrimination that prevailed because of a contract and not his qualifications. Arnie felt betrayed by the Union.

Arnie's troubles with employment did not end yet. By some formal definition, the economy had rebounded out of recession. For the common individual, nevertheless, the economy was anything but out of recession. Employers still wary of hiring, conducted mass layoffs anytime a whiff of negative forecast popped up. After five months of working on the $11 an hour job, and with just one month away from the contractually obligated Union protection, Arnie was summarily terminated.

Unemployed once again, Arnie wearily resumed the search for another job. By this time, he cultivated a substantial extent of negative view about Unions and bemoaned their increasing weakness on the subject of contract negotiations. This spawned another collateral damage. Arnie acutely despised anyone who was employed under the umbrella of Union protection. As a self-described pragmatic and rational individual, Arnie was surprised – sometimes startled - at his own emotions. Therefore, he made a conscious effort to erase what seemed to be an unjustified and childish hostility toward anything and anybody associated with the Union.

Finally, in July of this year, Arnie's roller coaster ride on the employment train caught another break. He received an offer of employment for a full time position with benefits. Arnie therefore bore justifiable levels of both excitement and relief. The latest job offered stronger prospects of remaining employed long term which in a way correlated to an improving economy. The compensation – $22.30 an hour - was higher than what Arnie earned at his last stable job, and substantially higher than any of the sporadic jobs he held in the past three years. To top it off, a Union represented his new position with a strong and favorable contract. Arnie truly hoped this would be the job where he would be able to dig in for the long haul. He also, in all sincerity, wished his detrimental attitude toward the Union and its employees would fade away and make him a better man over time.

Now with the middle of October well underway, Arnie had successfully completed almost three months at his new job. He enjoyed his work and the empowerment he believed he possessed. However, much to his own dismay, his silly bouts of animosity toward Unions never faded away in entirety; instead it reared its ugly head on more than a few occasions. He dismissed them as some random and normal ill-effect due to the past long bouts of unemployment he had endured. He referred to them as his own post-traumatic stress disorder.

~~~   6   ~~~

John Wharton was seated near Gate B21 at the Detroit Metropolitan Wayne County Airport waiting to board Delta flight 4613 to Houston, Texas. The CRJ900 aircraft, scheduled to depart at 8.55 am on this Monday morning of October 29th was lined up at the jet bridge for its first of many flights for the day. John would reach Houston around 11.15 am Central time. He had another hour to kill before departure. In the meantime, the usual and mysterious frenzy near the podium at the gate had begun with the passengers lined up and waiting to speak with the airline's agent.

John's trip to Houston entailed a crucial discussion with one of the suppliers which contributed more than its share of problems on the project he managed. He carried the unenviable role of forcing the supplier team to meet impractical deadlines imposed by the customers - in this case, Milamek Corporation and the end customer. A number of emails flew between the supplier and the Milamek's team with glaring evidence of heightened tension, friction, and disagreements between the parties. Evidently, people had discovered the convenience of hiding behind the laptops and type whatever came to their mind regardless of how these write ups would be perceived or misunderstood by the other party. When, however, the moment arrived for a face to face meeting, everyone behaved or pretended to behave like normal professionals. Of course, it was a matter of debate whether or not it was better to simply spit and punch each other when they met in person just to get the point across. John was scheduled to return on Wednesday, the Halloween day, on Delta flight 5827. He would be back by five pm which would allow him to get home to join his twins for the 'trick-or-treat' around the neighborhood that night.

Rakesh Jaiteley started the day with an international conference call. He was home in his pajamas. One of the hidden perks of employment at Milamek Corporation was the ability to, on occasion, work from home;

especially those employees whose roles did not have a direct impact on the day-to-day operations of the firm's manufacturing facilities. Rakesh's position called for his interaction with the engineers and designers at sites throughout the globe. This was in most cases achieved through phone and video conferences.

This morning, the phone call began at seven am Detroit time. The participants included the Sales group from Poland and a manufacturing plant from Southern China. Milamek Corporation had an Engineering, Sales, and Marketing Center in Poland in the city of Poznan. The ESM Center, as the location was referred to, handled the coverage of design, sales, marketing, and customer service for Europe and parts of Northern Africa. The city of Poznan situated in the west-central region of Poland along the river Warta was now the fifth largest city and among the oldest in Poland. The manufacturing plant in Southern China was on the outskirts of Shenzhen, a major metropolitan area just across the border from Hong Kong. The city of Shenzhen in Guangdong province hosted one of the busiest container ports in China. A number of crossing points between Shenzhen and Hong Kong existed, with an excess of two hundred thousand people using them every day in each direction.

The conference call progressed in the same predictable course as it almost always did. The Poles were livid at the Chinese for delivering parts of inferior quality, and the Chinese were livid at the Poles for failing to provide adequate lead time to deliver the parts. Rakesh listened, interjected, translated, moderated, and mediated the telephone discussion. However, after an hour of listening to the Poles and the Chinese argue with each other in English, Rakesh became hungry and ached for breakfast. He poured himself a bowl of Chocoroos and soaked them to the brim with cold whole milk. He muttered under his breath when the cereal pebbles, too light to sink in the milk, began to spill over the bowl. Being an experienced and efficient bachelor, Rakesh discovered the cereal to be the most heartfelt breakfast with the least time investment. The Chocoroos happened to be his latest cravings which he recently found at the grocery chain, Meijer, in the economy bulk pack section.

By nine am, Rakesh was on the highway headed to his office. He fidgeted with his phone calendar to check the day's meetings. His first one was scheduled at ten am followed by three more spread through the day. The two o'clock meeting which recurred every Monday was the worst. Vinita Grewal, the Divisional Head of Quality chaired the two pm meeting. Vinita, a perfect 'diversity' candidate in the eyes of the corporate human resources – female and Asian-American – held a leadership position which placed her right at the top of the Division's food chain. She commanded a number of solid and dotted line reports while she reported to none other than the Vice President of the Business group, a group which included few more Divisions of Milamek Corporation.

For Rakesh and the rest of the employees who were mandated to attend Vinita's weekly meeting, it was a matter of dread and misery. Her meetings always exceeded the allocated one hour and worse, she had very little propensity to listen, for, she loved to hear her own talking. This inevitably meant the attendees endured more than an hour of incoherent and rambling monologue filled with utter nonsense of complex sounding business speak. During her meetings, Vinita thrived on PowerPoint presentations and charts. The contents however, did nothing but insult the powerful software applications. In most cases, numerous, painfully obvious disconnect prevailed between the charts and her description of those charts. Among the attendees were five lucky ones who called in remotely from another Milamek location. These five enjoyed the coveted opportunity to simply mute the phone and do something else. Meanwhile, the Managers in the meeting room with Vinita kept to themselves in the hopes of ending the meeting sooner, but that almost always never happened. In the end, they all simply tolerated Vinita Grewal's one hour misery that she titled, 'Quality Trends Meeting'.

With John Wharton out of town, Rakesh offered to bring pizza for dinner for the twins and Karen, thereby saving her from the chore of cooking. Today was also Karen's parent-teacher day and she had several appointments, with the first one at one pm, and the last one ending at seven pm. Rakesh offered to 'baby-sit' the twins in their home while Karen finished up her parent-teacher meetings. Karen unhesitatingly accepted the offer.

The time was quarter to noon. The students at the Hadley Lyons Elementary were being dismissed and the organized pandemonium spread everywhere. The school monitors, bus monitors, and other staff assisted the children to their respective exits. A number of kids also stayed back until their parents and guardians arrived to complete the parent-teacher meeting, and few were escorted to the school's aftercare. Karen Wharton scheduled the parent-teacher appointments at thirty minute intervals. This facilitated a fifteen to twenty minute face time and another ten to wrap up and prepare for the next one. Typical of any public school system, the interest and involvement level of the parents varied from one end of the spectrum to the other, although at Hadley

Lyons Elementary, a majority of the parents showed an appreciable level of interest and curiosity about their little ones.

Few minutes before one pm, John Wharton called Karen to let her know of his safe arrival into Houston. After a short exchange of pleasantries and small talk, Karen hung up the phone to head for her first appointment. Karen's one pm was with Keisha Russell, mother of Jordon Russell, a talkative and a very sociable kindergartener. While Karen briefed Keisha, Jordan switched on one of the classroom computers, logged in, and dived into some interactive educational game. After completing the first two appointments, Karen left her classroom and returned with a cup of water. She checked the clock and took note of the ten minutes she still had before the next appointment at two pm. She walked over to the file cabinet and removed the files of her two o'clock student.

A couple of minutes before two o'clock, Brian Pratt walked into Karen's classroom with his kindergarten daughter, Makenzie. Karen Wharton greeted them both. Makenzie displayed an air of confidence at the sight of her familiar classroom, said hello to Ms. Wharton, and proceeded to find one of many recognizable play items that lay organized inside the room. Karen reminded Makenzie to shelve the items back in their place once she finished playing with them, and Makenzie nodded.

Meanwhile, Brian awkwardly settled himself on one of the tiny chairs which belonged to the students and noticed the stack of what appeared to be his daughter's work of crafts, writings, drawings, and math exercises. He also found other files and reports on the table. Karen began her assessment with a highly positive feedback of the child's personality and academic performance, all of which, needless to say, made Brian proud.

Rakesh's dreaded two o'clock meeting with Vinita Grewal was well underway. With most of the attendees tuned out by now, Rakesh spent his time concocting a number of possible excuses to quit attending future meetings. As a matter of fact, he hoped for an emergence of some miraculous excuse in order to walk out of today's meeting. One of the Managers seated in the last row of the meeting room took this time as an opportunity for a well-deserved manicure. The loud and incessant clicking of the nail clipper amused the rest of the attendees. Another Manager reviewed her emails on her phone. As Rakesh looked around, there were a couple others staring intently at their laptops browsing the internet, oblivious to Vinita's high pitched monologue. Meanwhile, Vinita remained equally oblivious to her attendees' total disregard and inattention. She never slowed down on her rambling which now centered on something about the cost of poor quality. The PowerPoint slide on the projector screen showed a bunch of bar charts indicating poor supplier performance.

Rakesh absorbed the dynamics of his meeting room ecosystem until something caught his attention. He noticed a co-worker reading the main page of CNN's website. On the top section of the web page, the most recent breaking news showed up. He leaned forward from his chair to get a better view of what that might be. The bold white letters on a black background read, 'Shooting reported at a Detroit area public school. More to follow.'

~~~   7   ~~~

Rakesh's curiosity edged up a notch. Better yet, he discovered a reason to distract himself away from the grueling meeting. Hurriedly, he opened the web browser on his phone and scanned for any details regarding the shooting. He typed in the address of Detroit's WDXZ website; he hoped to find more details on the local media than he did on CNN. He indeed found something and what he read raised his anxiety. The website stated that a shooting had occurred at a public school in the Beniton Heights school district about fifteen or twenty minutes ago. The news page did not carry any further information. The very reference of Beniton Heights was sufficient to stir up Rakesh. Unclear on what to perceive of the emerging news, he excused himself from the meeting, returned to his office, and rushed to open the internet browser on his laptop to search for anything he might be able to find.

While at his desk, Rakesh left the web pages open, and pored over the numerous and the unending barrage of corporate emails. Universal abhorrence against simple phone calls or face-to-face discussions appeared to be prevalent; even trivial messages from others who were situated no more than twenty feet away were exchanged via email. Amid the electronic communication, Rakesh continued to periodically survey the internet for any further development. Within the next ten minutes, few more details emerged on the websites of WDXZ and other major news outlets.

The shooting had occurred at Hadley Lyons Elementary School. Sufficiently alarmed, Rakesh's heart sank. He wondered about the whereabouts of Karen Wharton. The twins were at the school as well, waiting for him to pick them up in the evening. Rakesh wondered if John Wharton, in the midst of his contentious meeting in Houston, learned anything yet regarding this breaking news. Rakesh pulled out his phone and started dialing John's number to least alert him. He changed his mind however, hung up, and decided not to let John get worked up over information which appeared incomplete.

Incomplete news or not, Rakesh decided it would be prudent to contact Karen, and ensure the wellness of her and the two boys. Rakesh dialed Karen's cell phone and waited for her to answer. After six rings, the voicemail kicked in. Rakesh assumed Karen might be busy, either in the middle of her several meetings or distracted by the news of the shooting at her own school. Rakesh attempted to get in touch with Karen by sending her a couple of text messages. He hoped she would, at the minimum, respond with brief words of assurance.

By now, the clock showed three-fifteen in the afternoon. Every one of Rakesh's several more near frantic calls and texts went unanswered by Karen. Rakesh called the school, but the phone line returned the busy tone. He somewhat expected this as anxious parents and families were probably reacting and attempting to reach someone within the school premises. Rakesh dialed Karen's home number and the voicemail kicked in after three rings which did not surprise him a bit as she was not scheduled to return home until late evening.

According to media's latest information, the shooting resulted in injuries and fatalities at Hadley Lyons Elementary although none of them, at this time, had an inkling of how many. The media, however, did know this - the unfortunate event occurred around two-fifteen; the first responders arrived at the school property within three minutes after the first 911 call, and the SWAT teams continued to pour in. The updates indicated a deteriorating scenario at Hadley Lyons Elementary. Rakesh's anxiety escalated. Karen had not returned any of his messages. He remained unsure whether John was aware of these developments or if Karen had contacted John. Neither John nor Rakesh had contacted each other yet. With communication lacking, Rakesh decided he couldn't remain at work and speculate; rather, he needed to head over to the school and determine the latest status. More importantly he had to find Jake, Josh and Karen.

Once again, Rakesh contemplated contacting John Wharton and once again decided not to. His self-confidence assured him of his unwavering ability to provide any necessary support to handle the situation. Besides, while in Houston, John had limited means to do anything substantial other than worry. Rakesh drove out of the employee parking lot as he tried his best to remain calm. He realized that the incident at Hadley Lyons Elementary did not produce any positive outcome and was cognizant of the likelihood of high levels of confusion around the school campus. He was mentally prepared to face what he might find and told himself to stay determined and calm. Regardless, not knowing the whereabouts of Karen, Jake and Josh kept Rakesh's anxiety level at its maximum.

A few minutes before four o'clock, Rakesh arrived a mile away from Shaver Road as he drove on Macomb Line Road. He had his radio tuned to a news station, anxious to stay updated on the latest. What he heard continued to be grim. There were five dead and a small but unknown number of injured with the nature of the injuries uncertain. According to the reporter on the radio, the law enforcement authorities attributed the relatively minimal casualties to the early dismissal of the school. The officials estimated a presence of around eighty or so faculty, staff, and students at the time of the shooting. Most were by now evacuated; however, a few were possibly missing or not yet accounted for. While the officers tried to track those individuals down, the details of the perpetrator remained unknown at this time. In addition, no one had yet established if the killing involved more than one shooter.

From his location on Macomb Line Road, Rakesh witnessed the seriousness of the situation that continued to unfold near the school campus. All forms of emergency vehicles zipped back and forth on Macomb Line Road and were lined up along Shaver Road. While Macomb Line Road was open to traffic, the presence of numerous flashing lights and sirens slowed the vehicles down significantly. On the other hand, only emergency and law enforcement had access to Shaver Road. The residents of the homes on Shaver were either evacuated or denied entry for an indefinite period of time. One of the unknowns was whether the shooter was alive, dead, or on the run. In addition, the law enforcement had to confirm the number of shooters without any ambiguity.

Several news crews lined up along Macomb Line Road and more appeared to be converging. Rakesh figured it would be futile to sit in the car and attempt to get any closer; consequently, he drove into the parking lot of Macomb Outlets shopping complex at the corner of Shaver and Macomb Line. He parked his car and treaded the three hundred or so feet toward Shaver Road on foot. As he walked at a brisk pace, Rakesh noted several others doing the same. All had worried expressions; few worked their cell phones while others had their phones glued to their ears speaking in shaky and near panic voices. Some were in tears. Among those in tears that Rakesh noticed was a young woman pushing a stroller with a fast asleep toddler in it. Rakesh briefly glanced at her again.

~~~   8   ~~~

Anticipating the crowd of worried and panicked people, the police had set up a perimeter and stationed few officers in and around the parking lot. They directed the unrelated public away, kept the media personnel at bay, and provided guidance to those affected by the violence that had occurred a little over two hours ago. Rakesh approached one of the officers and disclosed the reason behind his presence. The officer pointed toward a recycling shed inside the shopping complex and explained that it served as the staging area for the evacuees. The school campus, by now, had been evacuated. The law enforcement and emergency personnel had deployed a hastily concocted protocol in which a positive identification of the adults allowed their departure while all unaccompanied children required a family member to arrive before their release. Rakesh thanked the officer and walked toward the shed.

The recycling shed was a ten thousand square foot climate controlled enclosure attached to the Macomb Outlets complex. Three dock doors allowed for the loading and unloading of the recycle trucks. Today, the shed was easily identifiable due to the presence of a number of police personnel in and around it. When Rakesh approached the building, someone directed him to a side door which was being used exclusively for entry. Another door served as an exit for people leaving the shed. This one way entrance and exit facilitated the school staff and emergency personnel to ensure the identity of anyone entering and exiting the shed. Besides, it provided some semblance of order in the time of chaos.

At the entrance, two heavily armed officers from the State Police asked for some form of identification. After proving his identity, Rakesh walked into the shed, paused, and peered around to get his bearings. Unsure of what he might encounter or expect, he remained tentative in his movements. Sensing a stranger's presence, a female school staff member flanked by two armed police officers greeted Rakesh. The staff member once again verified Rakesh's identity and asked the reason for his presence. Rakesh mentioned Karen and her boys' names. Needless to say, the staff member wanted to know how he was related to the three. Rakesh provided an elaborate explanation of his ties to the Wharton family, all of which were patiently listened to, duly questioned, verified, and re-verified by the police officers. The staff member then directed Rakesh to a designated location that served as a waiting area while she communicated something to other staffers via her two-way radio.

Rakesh walked toward the location inside the shed and scouted the area with his eyes. In one section of the shed, he found a number of students seated on the floor in straight rows interjected by an adult staff member. The students appeared visibly disconcerted, and as anxious as the outsiders searching for their beloved ones. The students had been lined up and seated according to their grades in order to enable proper traceability. In another section of the shed, another group of children sat with their parents. Rakesh assumed these to be the parents who were at the parent-teacher meeting at the time of the shooting. He chose this group and scanned the individuals' faces looking for Karen and the twins. They weren't to be found.

After a few moments of waiting anxiously, Rakesh noticed the twins walking toward him accompanied by a staff member. Rakesh felt an immense sense of relief as he rushed to greet the twins. The moment Jake and Josh spotted Rakesh, they ran toward and hugged him tight. With the twins shaking, Rakesh fought off his own whelming emotion. "Mr. Rakesh, we can't find mommy. Do you know where she is?" Jake, one of the twins, blurted out with abundant anxiety.

Perturbed, Rakesh turned to the staff member and hoped for an answer, but he received none. The staff member instead directed Rakesh to another section of the shed manned by a male staff and few more police personnel. At this section, the male staff member spoke to the twins for few seconds ascertaining some information and then asked the trio to take a seat. Amid the evacuation spree, someone had brought in chairs from somewhere and they lay around in a haphazard manner. The staff member had a hurried but a hushed conversation with another person for several minutes before returning his attention to Rakesh. He approached Rakesh and somberly announced Karen Wharton was missing and not accounted for, yet. Confused, Rakesh pressed for further clarification. Softly, the staff member explained that thirteen adults and six children had not yet been found or identified. He also confirmed the news reports Rakesh had heard earlier - five people died in the shooting; four adults and a child. The investigators had not yet identified the dead, and delayed the release of the information pending further investigation. The injured were admitted at the Beniton Heights General Hospital, although no one was allowed to visit them. The staff member did not have any details of the injured or the extent of the injuries; instead, he offered Rakesh the choice to either leave with the twins and be contacted later with information regarding Karen, or wait at the recycling shed until further details regarding the missing and the deceased became available. For now, Rakesh decided to wait. He became desperate to know what befell Karen.

By now, a very worried Rakesh determined that the twins would be his immediate priority and he would sort everything else one at a time. He had to be there for the twins and he would do anything to keep them calm and collected. He walked back a few steps toward the boys and sat next to them. The twins, although calm on the outside, appeared tense and remained unusually quiet. Rakesh explained to the twins that the emergency folks worked to track down all the missing people and they'll soon find their mom. In any event, Rakesh found unable to console the twins that everything would be okay – he had scant confidence that everything was indeed okay.

Rakesh sat there with Jake and Josh, with nothing to do but ponder about the past couple of hours. He tried to strike a conversation with the boys. But the boys seemed too distracted to talk; besides, he himself was not in any mood for a conversation. He asked if the twins were hungry and they nodded no. He looked around and saw nothing but grim faces in the crowd that constantly swelled and ebbed as more people came in to collect their loved ones. Few stayed back to find their missing while others left with a huge relief after having found their family member.

Rakesh then caught sight of the young woman with the stroller whom he had seen earlier in the parking lot. She was seated on the floor in the shed with her toddler and weeping quietly. No other children or adult accompanied her which indicated someone from her family was still missing. Her weeping unsettled Rakesh.

~~~   9   ~~~

Rakesh dialed Karen's cell phone few more times as he waited in the shed with the twins. She did not answer any of his calls. He sent her a few text messages, but received no response. He finally decided to call John Wharton. He figured that John's meeting would be over by now. Rakesh mentally prepared a script on how to break the news to John.

John picked up the phone after two rings.

"Hey man, how are you?" John sounded cheerful, and for no fault of his, appeared to have chosen a misplaced emotion, considering the unraveling situation far away from his current location.

"I am alright. How's Houston and how's the meeting?" As he asked, John's cheerfulness jolted Rakesh a bit, but soon realized John remained clueless about the shooting at Hadley Lyons. The twins, in the meantime, became aware that their dad was on the phone and wanted to speak with him. Rakesh, with a nod of his finger, asked them to wait until he was done talking.

"Same old shit. The meeting, that is." John laughed heartily as he replied. "We were all 'professional' to each other and didn't accomplish squat. The meeting is over and they are taking me to dinner tonight. Maybe I should go get drunk and give this piece of crap supplier whatever they want. At least, somebody will be happy. Oh yeah, Houston is spectacular, at least it is warmer than Detroit."

"Uh-huh." Rakesh paused. "John, are you someplace by yourself?"

"Yes, I am. I am in the conference room here wrapping up my stuff. What's the matter? You sound like someone's dead," chided John.

"Listen, I have a bit of bad news."

"Bad news? What's up?" John exuded more of curiosity than seriousness.

"A shooting happened at Hadley Lyons this afternoon, but…"

"A what? Shooting? What the hell are you talking about? You mean at Karen's school? Shit. Are the…."

43

"John, please, let me finish. Yes, it happened at Karen's school. The boys are ok. I am with them at an evacuation center which the cops have set up. It's a shed, you know, inside Macomb Outlets. Listen, I have one more thing. Karen is missing and ..."

"What do you mean missing? Were people killed? When did this shit happen?"

"Yes, the cops are saying five people are dead, one of them is a child. It's in the news all over the place. They are not...."

"Rakesh, what about Karen? What do you mean missing? When did all this happen?

"John, there are eighteen or twenty people still missing and the cops have not tracked them yet or at least they are not telling us. I am trying to find out where Karen is. That's why I am here waiting for more information. They also said people have been hurt, but the news is just trickling in and things are little confusing right now." A long discomforting silence persisted on the other end.

"John, are you there? Are you okay?" Even as Rakesh asked, the twins, clearly disturbed, despite being able to listen to only one side of the conversation, fidgeted and demanded Rakesh's attention. Rakesh pulled them closer and put his arm around their shoulder to comfort them.

"John, are you alright?" Rakesh asked again.

"Rakesh, do you think Karen got shot?" John asked in a shaky voice.

"I don't know John. Listen, I am going to stay with the boys for as long as I need to and find out where Karen is. Can you..."

"Who did this?"

"What?"

"Who shot these people? How soon can we find out about Karen?"

"John, I am trying to find out what happened to Karen." Rakesh lowered his voice. "I don't want to worry the boys more than they are at the moment, okay? So, I don't want to ramble on without knowing much. I need you to do one thing. Find the next available flight and get back home."

"Shit! It's almost five o'clock over here. I am not sure if I'll have enough time to get to the airport even if there is a flight. Let me check. The airport is thirty miles away and the goddamn traffic is worse than Detroit. Can I speak to the boys?"

"Yeah, of course." Rakesh handed the phone to Josh.

Josh took the phone, said hello, and promptly burst into tears. Jake followed suit. The boys released all their pent up anxiety and tension into tears. Rakesh began losing his composure himself and tried hard to stay calm. He grabbed the boys and held them closer. After a minute or so with the boys, John was back with Rakesh.

"Holy shit! This is bad. Rakesh, will you take care of the boys?" John asked. Rakesh perceived John's anxiety in his voice. So far however, John had absorbed the news relatively well and that was a relief for Rakesh.

Before Rakesh could answer, John chimed in. "Rakesh, gosh, what the hell will I do if I lose Karen? C'mon, I can't imagine how I can go on with…."

"John, stop, please stop. We are not sure of anything. I am going to find out where Karen is. You need to stay calm and try to get a flight back home, okay?"

"Alright, I am going to try. Call me as soon as you know something. I am going to keep calling you. Goddamn, this is bad."

Before he hung up, John said, "Rakesh, thanks for taking care of everything."

Rakesh told the twins to stay put and approached one of the officials to inquire once again about Karen. The official promised a decent update soon. He also stated they now knew more regarding the events and waited for further confirmation before proceeding to share with the affected families who were all still waiting in the shed. Amid the torrent of thoughts, Rakesh wondered if Karen indeed ended up as one of the victims of the shooting. He just could not pull himself to consider the plain possibility that Karen might be one of the five fatalities.

Rakesh brushed away his thoughts, looked around, and searched for the young woman with the toddler. He found her still seated on the floor where he saw her a few minutes earlier. She held and coddled her toddler, a little girl who was whimpering and restless. The woman stopped crying, at least that's how it appeared to Rakesh; rather, seemed to be in a daze waiting to hear about someone who apparently was missing or unaccounted for. Rakesh assumed that the woman was here seeking her missing child. He wondered where her husband was. Was he out of town as well? Was she a single parent? For some strange reason, Rakesh experienced a strong bout of sympathy for this young woman. He had an urge to walk over and offer her, at the least, some form of conversational support; however, he wasn't sure how she would react or if that was even appropriate. In the end, he decided not to interfere by justifying that he was a total stranger to her. More importantly, he had his mind full trying to figure out the situation with Karen. Yet, by all accounts, Rakesh felt lame regarding his own justification.

~~~   10   ~~~

With the passage of time and as evening fell, more children and adults departed the building. The recycling shed became quieter with only few left - presumably, acquaintances of those still declared missing or injured. The hospital with the injured still remained off-limits to the media and the families. The news outlets tirelessly replayed the same content; however, the dead were not yet identified. The officials wanted to ensure that the families knew first before the media did. This caused those remaining in the shed to hold a deep hope on the wellbeing of their family member.

In the meantime, John Wharton called Rakesh several times and became increasingly agonized at the lack of information regarding Karen's whereabouts. In his latest phone call, John informed he had just boarded a flight to Atlanta after a mad rush to the airport. Delta had promised to accommodate him on the first set of available flights from Atlanta to Detroit. For now, the airlines offered him a connection to Detroit via Minneapolis and John expected to be home thirty minutes past midnight.

The young woman with the toddler stood up as three people approached her. Among the three, one was the Principal of the school, Mrs. Kristine Hamilton, who spent the entire time in the shed dealing with the tragedy. The other two were a female officer from the Michigan State Police - Trooper Eileen McDougall, and a crisis counselor from the Oakland County Social and Welfare Administration. Trooper McDougall quickly grabbed four chairs and set them in front of the young woman while offering a chair for her. The toddler paid little attention to the latest gathering of strangers as she continued to play with something she found on the floor.

Despite the lack of privacy in the shed, Rakesh was unable to hear the conversation among the three officials and the young woman. In any event, it became distressingly obvious to him they were about to deliver very bad news to the young woman, and he could not bear the thought of the grief this woman would now endure. The Principal, Mrs. Hamilton, chosen to be the one to speak to the young woman, went to great lengths to be as gentle and sensitive as possible. With a soft voice, Mrs. Hamilton told the woman that her husband and daughter had been killed in the shooting.

Both Makenzie Pratt, the kindergarten student, and her father, Brian Pratt, died from gunshot wounds few hours ago while at the parent-teacher meeting with Karen Wharton.

Upon hearing this, the young woman placed her hands on her face and sobbed uncontrollably. She began losing whatever remained of her composure real fast. As the woman began to collapse in an apparent state of shock, Mrs. Hamilton hurriedly reached over and held her tight. The police officer and the crisis counselor jumped in right away and assisted Mrs. Hamilton hold the woman. The woman mumbled something incoherently, but her sobs drowned the words. The crisis counselor attempted to calm the young woman down; the futility of it was conspicuous by the woman's overwhelming grief. The toddler witnessed the complete breakdown of her mother and began wailing. Trooper McDougall held the child and tried her best to console the little girl; this only confused and scared the child who wanted nothing but be with her mom. Meanwhile, the young woman was in no state to hold her toddler or handle much of anything other than pour her grief on Mrs. Hamilton's shoulder in an endless stream of tears.

Rakesh observed the young woman's immense outpouring of grief with a deep sense of helplessness. From his location, he couldn't tell who the young woman had lost, but that was irrelevant. He somehow sensed the woman lost the only person or people she cherished the most in her life. Rakesh found unable to fathom himself in a similar situation. Finding his own tears welling up, he fought hard to regain composure. Rakesh was determined to stay strong for the sake of the twins. He could not afford to lose his emotions, not now.

Then, in a gut wrenching moment, Rakesh realized the twins had bad news waiting for them. Only a few minutes passed before Rakesh noticed three women approaching him and the twins. One of them was the School District Administrator, Dr. Pamela Temple. The other two - county's crisis counselors - gently insisted they take the twins to another section of the shed, and Rakesh meekly consented. The fact Rakesh was not an immediate family member of the twins somehow made it easier for Dr. Temple to discuss the horror of the day's gun violence in a lot more detail than what she normally would have. Without mincing her words, Dr. Temple told Rakesh that Karen Wharton was killed by a single shot in the neck during the parent-teacher meeting.

Rakesh stared at Dr. Temple in dead silence. At a loss for words, his determination and mental preparation to remain strong failed him. He sensed his mouth turn dry and tears run down the face. He quickly put his head down and wiped the tears off. Dr. Temple placed her hands on his shoulder in an attempt to console him. Despite his own shock, Rakesh realized that John Wharton would be the one who would need all the consolation in the world, as he would never his wife alive again.

With a heavy lump in his throat, he looked at Dr. Temple and turned his attention to the corner where the counselors had the twins. The twins had their backs against Rakesh; therefore, he had no way of ascertaining what the twins were going through. His thoughts drifted back to John. What would he tell him? How would he tell him? Rakesh bore no clue. It seemed to be only a matter of time before John would call from Atlanta or whichever connecting airport he might be transiting through at the moment. Should Rakesh hold off until John arrived in Detroit? Dr. Temple seemed to sense Rakesh's predicament and inquired the whereabouts of the twins' father. Rakesh told her. They then proceeded to identify the best means to notify John.

At this point, Dr. Temple went further and informed Rakesh that a father and her daughter who were with Karen at the meeting were also killed. The earlier reports of injuries turned out to be highly unreliable and mostly minor. Most injuries seemed to have occurred as people rushed to get out amid the pandemonium. All the missing had been tracked, identified, and accounted. Most of the missing either drove away in an effort to get out of the campus or ran and hid in the backyards of the residences on Shaver Road.

Upon learning of the deaths of the other two in Karen's class, Rakesh pointed to the young woman and asked Dr. Temple if those two were related to the woman. Dr. Temple expressed reluctance to divulge the information; in the end however, she revealed the relationship between the young woman and the two deceased. Dr. Temple did not mention anyone's names and Rakesh did not press further. However, with the media continuing to report latest developments, it was only a matter of time before Rakesh would learn the names of Brian and Makenzie. Rakesh looked in the direction of the young woman and saw Mrs. Hamilton still trying her best to comfort her. The young woman seemed inconsolable.

After several minutes of conversation with Rakesh, Dr. Temple excused herself, as she had to attend to few other families. Rakesh sought the twins who needless to say, by now, had been told of their mother's fate. Rakesh's urge to interrupt and take the boys home heightened, but he held it off and waited for the crisis counselors to complete their work.

Rakesh called his Manager and briefed him of the tragic situation. The two men had a hurried conversation and then decided to contact the Human Resources as well as John's Manager. After a flurry of phone calls among the Managers and Human Resources, it was decided that the HR and John's Manager would meet John at the Detroit airport and inform him of his wife's death. They would arrange transportation for John and remain with him as long as it was necessary. Meanwhile, everyone tried to determine the exact time of John's arrival. John, in the meantime, had not called Rakesh in a while and Rakesh simply assumed he was either on the plane or busy finding his next available connection. Besides, despite the fact Rakesh had prepared himself to be the bearer of the bad news, he felt inadequately prepared for the situation, and remained unsure of how he would handle the call with John, if one materialized.

Amid all the confusion, phone calls, and discussions with the school officials, Rakesh still did not know the identity of the perpetrators. It did not matter anyway; the person who Rakesh cared about was dead and her family would now have to live with that fact. Dr. Temple did not provide any information about the shooter either. He checked the news on his phone and found none. With a pre-occupied state of mind, Rakesh pondered how to handle the situation with the twins and John for the next foreseeable several hours or maybe even days. Rakesh would most certainly support John with everything he had at his disposal while the formalities of caring for the deceased were handled.

At the time Karen and John left Morehead, they also left most of the family behind. The near and dear, along with the immediate and the extended family, lived in Kentucky, spread around Morehead, Louisville, and Lexington areas. While the Wharton couple had no regrets whatsoever on relocating to Beniton Heights, they did experience the loss of family support that was otherwise within a short driving distance. Rakesh concluded that by now the family might be at least aware of the shooting and were most likely attempting to get in contact with the Whartons.

~~~   11   ~~~

Rakesh turned his sight toward the young woman. The officer from the State Police, Trooper McDougall, had her arms around the woman while holding the toddler on her lap. Mrs. Hamilton and the crisis counselor were now speaking with someone else in another section of the shed. The young woman was still undoubtedly in tears while the toddler had calmed down and settled comfortably in the lap of the police officer. The child nibbled on some snacks fed by the officer. The young woman had both her feet up in the chair and was huddled in a fetal position. Neither the woman nor Trooper McDougall spoke to each other; they seemed to be lost in their own thoughts.

Rakesh was deeply perturbed that no one resembling family accompanied the young woman. He hoped, in the few hours which had elapsed since he first spotted her in the Macomb Outlets parking lot, someone would arrive in support of her. He detected none. A million reasons were possible for the woman's lone presence, including the likelihood her family lived elsewhere in the country, just as John and Karen's did. Still, something about the young woman continued to ruffle Rakesh's emotions.

Mired in his thoughts, Rakesh noticed the counselors approaching him with the twins. Rakesh hunched down and gave the twins a comforting hug. One of the boys said in a tearful voice, "Mr. Rakesh, mom is dead." At this, the second boy burst out in tears.

"I know, I know. It's going to be alright." Reassuring the boys in a gentle voice, Rakesh held them close as he despised himself for not being able to say much of anything else.

"Is dad coming back from Houston?" Jake exhibited palpable anxiety.

"Yes, he is. He is on his way."

"When will he be here? I want daddy," moaned Josh.

"He should be here by midnight. We'll go to my house for now and wait until your dad gets home, okay?"

Josh continued with his questions. "Where is he now? Why can't he be here sooner?"

"Your dad is trying to find flights and it's going to be a while before he gets in here."

"Does dad know what happened to mom?" Josh asked.

"No, someone from work will tell him when they bring dad from the airport."

"Will he be sad?" Jake asked.

"Yes, he will be… very much, just like you both are. But, it's okay to be sad. It will be alright."

"Mr. Rakesh, I miss mommy." Josh said with tears flowing down his face.

"Can we go find mommy?" Jake asked.

Rakesh told the twins they couldn't yet, since the authorities needed time to sort out. Of course, that did not convince either of the boys who insisted on finding their mother, wherever she might be. It took a bit of persistent talking on the part of Rakesh and the counselors before the twins calmed down.

Rakesh thanked the counselors and glanced around the shed, which by now had no more than thirty people, mostly law enforcement officers and few school staff, trying to wrap up things for the day. Rakesh eventually learned that Karen's remains would be released to the family after an autopsy which might take another twenty-four to forty-eight hours. With nothing else to look forward to on this grim evening, Rakesh decided to go home, be with the twins, and wait for John to return.

Trooper McDougall who was with the young woman determined that the grief stricken woman was in no condition to drive home by herself. Rakesh saw the officer assisting the traumatized young woman and her toddler into the police cruiser. Once again, Rakesh sensed a resounding urge to do something for the young woman; however, he was unsure of what that appropriate, tangible, and meaningful something would be. Rakesh got in his car with the twins as the police vehicle drove away with the young woman.

With a heavy heart and the persistent knot in his stomach, Rakesh drove home.

~~~ 12 ~~~

By daybreak the following day, the news outlets on the TV, radio, and the internet filled the airwaves, cable, and cyberspace with facts, speculation, theories, and conspiracies. Headline news channels replayed their footage on the screens in an endless stream while pundits commented and expressed anguish, surprise, and condemnation regarding gun violence in the United States. Amid the torrent of information and commentaries came the details of the shooter.

The investigators identified Arnie Casper as the gunman who murdered three adults and one five year old child before taking his own life.

In late last year and early this year, two other shooting incidents occurred at public school campuses – one in a middle school in Tucum, New Mexico and the other at an elementary school in Himer City, Utah. Both the events claimed the lives of more than thirty innocent children and elevated the profile of the otherwise quiet towns to an undesired level of infamy. As was the case each time, endless debates and arguments sprouted among the nation's populace which was bitterly divided along the ideological principles of gun control versus the absolute freedom to bear arms. The politicians vowed to do something, and as always, inaction triumphed for fear of backlash. Debates on enforcing the current laws and the need to enact new ones raged and fizzled. In the end, people's memory proved to be short; life went on, except for those who lost their children and loved ones in these senseless acts of violence.

Within these muddied waters emerged one federal level proposition which miraculously gained traction, won the support of the majority, and managed to be signed into law. The original proposal entailed enhancing safety at school campuses throughout the country. The seemingly simple phrase, 'enhancing safety' ended up being interpreted in a multitude of ways by the different interest groups, lobbyists and politicians. At one end of the spectrum, raising school safety was construed as, among other things, locking down schools during certain hours, improving video surveillance, ensuring the hiring of support staff by following extensive background checks, and requiring visitors to submit to additional checks before being allowed into the premises. At the other end of the spectrum, enhancing safety meant arming the teachers and placing well trained armed security personnel. The idea was to counter an armed bad guy with an equally armed good guy.

In the end, amid a current political environment where compromise held the prevalence of the unicorn, a compromise was indeed reached. Among the number of security enhancements implemented, one included placement of armed security officers within the school property, including inside the buildings. The guidelines on how many officers per school and the timeline to execute the plan were left to the individual States and the school districts. However, the school districts were strongly encouraged to have armed security in place before the beginning of the current academic year. In order to recruit motivated individuals to these positions, the Feds mandated the budget strapped State Governments to form a new bureaucracy that would monitor and regulate the individuals hired for these positions. The starting wage for these positions was set at $22.30, but the States were more than welcome to consider a higher wage if the individuals' prior experience and the States' own cost of living warranted it. Of course, the Federal Government would pitch in to help the States.

In the meantime, a well-known Union – the North American Labor Union (NALU) - which represented workers across major swaths of the United States and Canada entered the fray and somehow proclaimed itself to be the messiah for these future public school security officers. The Union executives also successfully botched any hopes of merit or experience based pay, resulting in a flat rate of $22.30 per hour for all security guards across the board. In the end, anyway anyone viewed, it became mighty clear that the taxpayers were the only ones on the hook for this massive recruitment.

Another point of debate in the safety enhancement saga was the type of weapon the security officers would carry. After contemplating every variety of arms available, some bureaucrat decided that these personnel would bear the same arms the police did.

Arnie Casper was hired in July of this year, along with Lewis Stratton, Reggie McNamara and Jimmy Hu, to form the four person security crew at Hadley Lyons Elementary school. All the four men cleared the rigorous background checks without any issues whatsoever and were slated to begin their tenure in the following month. Arnie's less than impeccable employment history came to light during the background check. However, he never lied during the interview and came clean with all of his gaps in employment. Considering the state of the country's economy, the interviewers accepted Arnie's lapses in the labor market. In addition, all the four security officers underwent a psychiatric evaluation as well as a physical exam. All of them passed both the exams with flying colors. Arnie's strange bouts of disdain for all things Union never came up, revealed or discussed during any of the exams, evaluations or checks.

On the day of the shooting, Arnie and Lewis patrolled inside the building while Reggie and Jimmy were outside monitoring the perimeter of the campus. Due to the dismissal of students at noon, at the time of the shooting, the building had only a few people within. A few minutes after two in the afternoon, both men were walking together inspecting the classrooms and chatting about nothing in particular. When the two approached Karen Wharton's kindergarten classroom, Arnie Casper pulled out his gun and without any warning or provocation, shot Lewis at close range killing him in an instant. Lewis Stratton became the first of the five casualties of the day's shooting. Before anyone in the vicinity could figure out what just happened, Arnie walked into Karen's classroom and shot Brian Pratt. He slumped on the floor from his tiny chair and died a few seconds later. As Karen looked up bewildered at what had just occurred, Arnie shot her as well and claimed his third victim. Makenzie Pratt, Brian's daughter and student of Karen, screamed and ran to her dad. Arnie pulled the trigger again claiming the life of the five year old.

At this point, Arnie either realized his disastrous folly or completely lost his nerves. In any case, he walked out of the classroom shaking and came face to face with Mr. Rhodes, the gym teacher. Mr. Rhodes had managed to move toward the source of the gunshots while the rest of the school occupants rushed to get out. Mr. Rhodes, a tall man with a build capable of tackling more than two grown men, had about a second or two to absorb the scene of the carnage and its perpetrator. In a fit of rage, he advanced toward Arnie with no care for his own safety. Mr. Rhodes however was immensely fortunate. Upon spotting the well-built man charging toward him, Arnie turned the gun on himself and ended his life. Mr. Rhodes frantically dialed 911, one of many that day.

It took a few minutes for Reggie and Jimmy to arrive at the source of the murders, and by that time, it was too late to do anything.

~~~   13   ~~~

The memorial service for Karen Wharton took place on November 1st followed by the funeral on November 2nd. A large gathering of family, friends, most of Hadley Lyons' teachers, and an appreciable number of kindergarten students and their families attended the service. In addition, several teachers from other schools of the Beniton Heights school district showed up to pay their respects. At the request of the family, the funeral was a private gathering of relatives and very few close friends. Rakesh attended both.

Watching John Wharton overwhelmed with grief was heartbreaking, and Rakesh hoped John would somehow find the strength to overcome his loss and move on, at least for the sake of his twin boys. In the midst of the loss, a comforting fact prevailed - John enjoyed an immense support of family, as evidenced by the presence of a large number of people from both sides of the family who had traveled from various regions of Kentucky. The family initially contemplated having the services in Morehead; however, decided against it due to John's concern on transporting Karen's remains several hours away.

Following Karen's funeral, Rakesh persisted in his curiosity about the young woman and her toddler. The last he saw her was when she was assisted by the State Police trooper in the parking lot outside the recycling shed. What intrigued him more about her was the fact that her husband and daughter happened to be with Karen at the parent-teacher meeting. After a prolonged agonizing, Rakesh concluded he needed to attend the funeral of the woman's husband and daughter. He felt he might be able to put his restless thoughts to rest if he reached out and made some form of connection to the young woman's loss. Of course, Rakesh had to first determine the identity of the young woman, plus the details of the funeral. Even if he learned of the details, if the funeral ended up being a private one, he might not be able to attend. In any case, to begin with, he decided to find out a few basic details.

Rakesh perused the news for any further details on funerals for individuals killed in the school shooting and found none. Apparently, by now, most of the national news outlets had moved on to other sensational stories which brought them further fame and ratings. A Detroit area news outlet carried a brief reference of the memorial and funeral service for Karen. In another section, a dedication was posted in remembrance of the young woman's daughter, Makenzie Pratt, as portrayed by her classmates. Besides that, Rakesh did not find anything.

After some thought, Rakesh contacted the School District Administrator, Dr. Pamela Temple, the individual who notified Rakesh of Karen's demise on the day of the shooting. Rakesh assured Dr. Temple he did not intend to be intrusive or disruptive; rather, he simply felt the need to mourn for the young woman who lost two of her loved ones. It took Rakesh several moments of convincing before Dr. Temple agreed - with reluctance - to find out if someone at Hadley Lyons Elementary was aware of the funeral arrangements for Brian and Makenzie. She promised to call him back later in the day.

With impatience, Rakesh waited for the call from Dr. Temple. The phone rang as the day neared its end. It was Mrs. Kristine Hamilton, the Principal of Hadley Lyons Elementary. She stated she was calling on behalf of Dr. Temple and right away made it clear she was at best, suspicious of his intent. In an attempt to revert her suspicion, Rakesh began by explaining his relationship with the family of Karen and therefore his presence at the school. He admitted he did not have a compelling reason to attend the funeral of the young woman's family other than the empathy for her. His lengthy and patient convincing appeared to work with the Principal.

Mrs. Hamilton mentioned that the woman's name was Lina Pratt. For the first time, Rakesh learned of her name. The toddler who was with Lina was Madeline Pratt, a two year old - an age too young to comprehend the loss of her father and big sister. Mrs. Hamilton affirmed herself as the one who broke the tragic news to Lina. Rakesh indeed remembered the three people, including the police officer, who spoke to Lina on the day of the shooting. The Principal stated she had kept in touch with Lina and therefore was aware of the funeral arrangements for Brian and Makenzie. She emphasized that Lina had requested a private funeral. Therefore, Mrs. Hamilton said, if Rakesh insisted on attending the funeral, he could only do so with her accompanying him. Grateful, Rakesh agreed to the proposal without any hesitation. According to Mrs. Hamilton, few other Hadley Lyons Elementary school teachers planned on attending as well.

The funerals for Brian and Makenzie were scheduled for the morning of November 7th at the Hemmann Green Crematorium. Rakesh found it a bit unusual at Lina's choice of cremation over a traditional cemetery. From a religious perspective, cremation continued to be the standard practice among the Hindus, Jains, Sikhs and the Buddhists. Among the Christian faith, cremation generally remained discouraged, although there now appeared to be wider acceptance among many denominations. Rakesh assumed that Lina might have chosen cremation based on her personal beliefs.

The Hemmann Green Crematorium, located on Shepherd Street six miles south of Hadley Lyons Elementary school in the city of Beniton Heights, bore peach colored walls with dark brown tiled roof. The apparent tropical decor meant to offer a soothing environment for the grieving. Rakesh learned that the funeral was set to begin at nine o'clock in the morning. He arrived at the crematorium at a time previously agreed between him and Mrs. Hamilton. Rakesh remained uncertain how his presence might be perceived by the family of the deceased; however, he figured things would be alright since he accompanied Mrs. Hamilton, whom Lina would recognize.

Rakesh spotted Mrs. Hamilton across the parking lot of the crematorium and prepared to step out of his car. Before he did, he picked up a sealed 9" x 4" standard envelope from the passenger seat of his car and put in his coat pocket. He walked over to Mrs. Hamilton, thanked her again for obliging to his request to attend the funeral.

Unlike the day of the shooting, Rakesh hoped and expected to see an appreciable number of family members. Upon entering the crematorium however, Rakesh became deeply disturbed to discover the family missing altogether, not to mention his startling surprise due to the presence of just a small number of people who perhaps numbered no more than a dozen to fifteen - a stark contrast to Karen's memorial service. Rakesh spotted Lina at the front of the group and she appeared too exhausted to cry anymore. Her daughter, Madeline, oblivious of her surroundings, was quite content at all the attention she received from the adults around her. Trooper McDougall from the State Police was present and she attended more in the capacity of an acquaintance who had come to know Lina since the shooting than as a law enforcement official. There were also perhaps five or six teachers from Hadley Lyons.

Besides these folks, Rakesh guessed the remainder might have been neighbors, co-workers or friends. From the looks of it all, it became abundantly obvious to Rakesh that no one in the crematorium was related to Lina or her deceased husband, Brian. This seemed to confirm what Rakesh suspected all along - neither Lina nor Brian appeared to have family members willing or able to support Lina at the time of this tragic loss. Needless to say, Rakesh had no idea why. He reached into his coat pocket and ensured the sealed envelope was still there. Maybe, he thought, after all it wasn't ridiculous of him to bring along the sealed envelope.

At nine o'clock, the Director of the crematorium escorted Lina and the rest of the group to the area where the cremation would be performed. This area allowed the mourners to witness the cremation process. The cremation chamber lay inside another room surrounded by glass windows. Laws mandated crematoriums to cremate one body at a time. The entire cremation process, from the start to the finish, consumed anywhere from two to three hours. As a result, today's funeral for the two was expected to consume the entire morning, if not more.

At the sight of the covered remains of Brian and Makenzie near the cremation chamber, Lina broke down sobbing. Mrs. Hamilton and the police officer instinctively moved next to her and consoled her as best as they could. The crematory operator, the individual assigned to perform the actual process of cremation, began the series of cremation steps by first completing positive identification of both the bodies and cross-checking with the records.

By early afternoon, the funeral ended. Per Lina's request, the crematorium handed the ashes of Brian and Makenzie Pratt to her in two separate urns which the crematorium itself had helped select. The small crowd of people approached Lina, said their condolences, and left. Rakesh stayed close to Mrs. Hamilton as he approached Lina to convey his condolences. Mrs. Hamilton said few words to Lina and she responded back in a halting manner while glancing at the Asian man whom she had never seen before. Mrs. Hamilton eventually introduced Rakesh to Lina. She told Lina that Rakesh was a family friend of Mrs. Wharton, Makenzie's kindergarten teacher. Lina nodded in silence as she wiped away the tears from her bloodshot eyes.

Rakesh stepped forward a bit and offered Lina his deepest condolences, and wished her and Madeline the best in finding solace and a path to move forward. He then pulled out the sealed envelope from his pocket and handed to Lina. Lina was clueless as to what this man handed her or why he did, but was in no emotional position to ask. Instead, she simply accepted the envelope, folded, and held it in her hands while looking questioningly at Rakesh and Mrs. Hamilton. Mrs. Hamilton was equally clueless.

On his drive back home, Rakesh truly hoped, that his note, as vague as it seemed, and that too from an absolute stranger, would be least intrusive while offering Lina some glimmer of hope if she so desired. But, Rakesh wasn't sure, and whatever might transpire remained to be seen.

~~~   14   ~~~

A few days passed before Lina Pratt opened the envelope, and found a handwritten note inside. The writing on the letter-sized paper read, 'My name is Rakesh Jaiteley. I am truly sorry for your terrible loss. If there is anything I can do to help, please do not hesitate to contact me. My phone number is.....' and the note ended with his phone number.

Not quite sure what to decipher of the message, Lina read it a few more times before placing the paper back in its envelope and tossing it on the computer desk in the corner study of her home. Lina did not have time to indulge in vague notes from strangers. She was now thrust into a forced circumstance which required her to manage and handle an overwhelming number of things in addition to caring for Madeline and working her job. On top of all, she had to pore over numerous items and identify the details of those; something Brian had taken care of, while he was alive. To make matters worse, she was unaware of the whereabouts of every piece of information, and when she did become aware, wasn't sure if she comprehended them to the fullest extent. All of this put Lina in a position in which she couldn't even afford the time to grieve for her lost daughter and husband. Amid her busy and chaotic state of affairs, she did not think much about Rakesh's note.

In the end, a few more days passed before Lina happened to chance upon the envelope that was on the computer desk where she had left it earlier. She opened it again and read several more times, but she still couldn't decode the person's intent, and therefore suspected a scam – such as the rest of the phone calls and mail that bombarded her on a regular basis. In any case, Lina vaguely recalled the person who had handed her the note and also remembered the fact that Mrs. Hamilton, whom she trusted, had accompanied him. As much as she tried, Lina failed to recall if she knew the man from any time in the past. Finally, Lina realized she was too curious and besides, the simplicity of the message bewildered her. In the end, Lina, filled with abundant wariness, hoped she had nothing to lose by contacting this Rakesh person.

Consequently, on the morning of Saturday, December 8th, Lina dialed Rakesh's phone number. No one answered and she did not leave a message. For the next few minutes, she contemplated her choices – either abandon the idea of contacting Rakesh or continue trying. Lina chose the latter and called again. This time Rakesh answered. Following a brief conversation, they decided to meet at the Beniton Heights public library.

THE SECOND PHASE

~~~   15   ~~~

The civic center branch of the Beniton Heights public library was located within the city's civic center complex. The complex consisted of several buildings and housed a myriad of public service departments. The Beniton Civic Park was located behind the complex. Within the park, several nature trails weaved around a golf course. The library occupied the first three floors of one of the ten floor buildings in the complex. The second floor of the library housed fifteen study rooms, any of which could be booked in advance by any resident of the city of Beniton Heights.

After the phone call from Lina on Saturday, exactly a week ago, Rakesh booked one of the study rooms for two hours. Both had agreed to meet on this day, December 15th, at the library at two o'clock, a time Lina had suggested since her two year old, Madeline, was usually on her afternoon nap schedule. Lina hoped this would allow her to have an undisrupted conversation.

Rakesh arrived at the library a half-hour early, approached the front desk staff, and re-confirmed his reservation for the study room. He looked forward to the meeting with Lina, although he couldn't predict the path or the outcome of the conversation. His note to Lina was conspicuous in its open-endedness; therefore, there was no way of telling what she had in mind for today. He tried to rehearse possible conversations as a means to be prepared, but eventually gave up. Preoccupied with a mix of thoughts, Rakesh wandered through the library aisles and without any purpose, flipped through the pages of randomly picked books. Around ten minutes before two o'clock, he walked back to the main lobby and settled on one of the couches facing the main entrance. He wanted to ensure both of them spotted each other effortlessly.

A couple of minutes passed before Rakesh spotted a young woman with a stroller walk through the sliding doors of the main entrance. In an instant, he recognized her as Lina Pratt. Madeline was fast asleep tucked in the stroller. Rakesh instinctively stood up and walked toward her. As he approached her, Lina noticed him as well. She did not quite recognize Rakesh, having seen him only once for a brief moment at the funeral; however, she guessed the man who approached her was indeed Rakesh. No one else was expecting her anyway.

As Lina walked toward him, she took note of his tall stature that sported a full and well groomed dark black mustache. Rakesh's thick black hair was cut conservatively. There were emerging traces of gray hair on the hairline along his temples. Rakesh was wearing a marine blue crew neck sweater on top of a solid off-white shirt along with savannah blue faded jeans and dark tan loafers. A black leather jacket slung over his left arm. Rakesh had a pleasant brown complexion. He was nothing of a fashion statement; nevertheless, he presented a first impression which was trustworthy enough for Lina to not turn around and walk away.

Rakesh found Lina to be in sharp contrast from the day of the shooting and the funeral when she was nothing but an inconsolable grieving young woman filled with tears and deep sorrow. Lina appeared to have recovered, at least from the outside, although he was sure she hadn't. He was relieved when he detected her ever so light, tentative smile as she approached him. When she was just a few feet away from him, her eyes caught his attention. She had irises of distinctly different colors. Her left eye was hazel while her right was brown. Rakesh had heard and read of people with different colored irises; however, had never met or seen one face to face. He quickly recalled the medical term for this condition – Heterochromia, which meant 'different colors'. Most cases of Heterochromia were hereditary and were caused by some genetic variation, disease or injury. In any case, Rakesh found her eyes pleasingly piercing and exotic. Lina had dark brown hair which she wore in a pony tail that trailed well below her shoulders and over her sepia brown woolen coat. Her hair on the sides was pushed behind her ears and she wore no visible jewelry.

Rakesh smiled gently, introduced himself, and extended his hands for a handshake. Lina reciprocated with a firm handshake. Rakesh mentioned the study room he had booked and escorted her upstairs via an elevator. The study room had a six foot wide elliptical table with five chairs around it. Rakesh and Lina picked a chair of their own and sat across from each other. Madeline was still fast asleep. The library had a 'no food, no drinks' policy, so Rakesh couldn't offer her anything other than the direction to the water fountain. Rakesh broke the few seconds of awkward silence between them.

"Madeline looks adorable. She is two, right?" Rakesh remembered the child's age from an earlier conversation with Mrs. Hamilton, the school Principal.

"Thanks. Yeah, she is, and a handful too." Lina replied with a smile. "Uh, thanks for agreeing to meet with me."

"Oh, that wasn't a problem at all. Let's hope something good comes out of this. So, how have you been?"

"Well, crazy busy, but okay so far. I miss my husband and daughter too much, but my busy schedule keeps me distracted."

Rakesh nodded gently in acknowledgement.

Rakesh took the lead once again to move the conversation ahead. "You probably have a lot of questions on your mind regarding my note. I just want to let you know a couple of things. One, any conversation today and maybe in the future is between us. I am not going to blabber to anyone about what you may share with me. Second, it's entirely up to you what you want to ask and tell. I do not and will not take any offense and I'll make sure not to become intrusive or make you uncomfortable. Uh, one more thing. You can ask any question and I'll try to answer as much as I can. Fair enough?"

"Sure, I appreciate it." Lina nodded in agreement.

Rakesh pointed toward the sleeping child. "How long does she sleep in the afternoon?" He attempted to enhance the ambience of their conversation.

"Uh, on weekends, she sleeps for more than three hours. She goes to a daycare on weekdays and they let all the kids sleep for two hours after lunch."

"That's right, I remember you saying you work full time, right?"

"Yeah, I work for a small private company in Royal Oak. Have you heard of Lennardin Corporation?"

"Uh, no, what do you do for them?"

"I am a graphics designer. We design and print all sorts of labels and tags for all sorts of products. A lot of times, we create custom designs for our customers and I am one of the two designers doing the work."

"That's cool. Do you like what you are doing?"

"Yes, I do. I started with them last summer. So far it's been great. They treat me well, but I am still new with them."

"Where did you work before that?"

"Oh, well, at lot of places." Lina let out a short burst of laughter as she replied. "We moved quite a bit after we got married. My employment history," she said rolling her eyes, "is filled with a lot of locations." Lina laughed again.

Lina abruptly switched topic toward a more personal question. "How old are you?"

"Too old." Rakesh chuckled as he replied. "Well, I am forty." After a pause, he said, "I guess I am past the hump, huh?"

Lina returned a polite smile before asking the next question. "Are you married?"

"Nope. I am a full time bachelor. Of course, which also means I am not left alone. My parents are quite persistent in reminding me many times."

Lina smiled. "It's not too bad being married. I got married young."

Rakesh was curious about her age and thought of asking. Instead, he replied, "I suppose it's not too bad. Well, I don't know. I just like it this way, I guess."

Lina nodded with a smile. There was a pause.

"So, Rakesh, really, why did you give me the note on that day?"

Rakesh took a deep breath as if to collect the proper choice of words before describing his reasons. "When I noticed you on the day the shooting happened, it seemed to me there was no one who could be with you. But I simply assumed a number of reasons for that. Anyway, I was bothered and I ended up insisting on attending the funeral. That's how I came upon Hadley Lyons's Principal, Mrs. Hamilton. My suspicion seemed to be right when I once again didn't find anyone with you at the funeral. So, I decided to hand you the note. I realized it was weird, but I felt better, knowing my note could serve some purpose."

Lina simply stared at him with those bright colored eyes for several seconds before answering. "Well, you guessed right. I don't have any family worthy of talking about."

Rakesh nodded in silence.

"I think, at the funeral, Mrs. Hamilton said something about you being related to someone in the school. Is that so?" Lina asked.

Rakesh briefly explained about his friendship with the Wharton family and what he was doing at the school on the day of the shooting. Lina was no stranger to Karen, either. Both Brian and Lina had met Karen a couple of times, once two weeks before the commencement of the academic year and another time a month or so into the school year. The first visit was part of the official introduction of the kindergarten teacher to the new batch of students and their parents. The second time was to meet Karen to discuss Makenzie's complaint regarding a classmate of hers. Both times, Karen proved to be an extremely pleasant individual to interact with, and Lina was pleased to have Mrs. Wharton as Makenzie's teacher. So, this afternoon, as Rakesh recalled Karen, Lina's memories of the day of shooting flooded back and her eyes welled up. She wiped her tears away.

Madeline stirred in her stroller. She turned her head to the left and curled up again into a deep sleep. Lina got up to check on her, adjusted her blanket, and returned.

Rakesh allowed Lina to settle back. "Lina, I realize you have a lot of things on your plate right now. Is there anything in particular, anything at all, I can help you with to make things easier for you?"

Lina looked at him. "Will you really help me if I ask?"

"Of course I will. I wrote and gave you the note, didn't I?"

"Ok, thank you." She sighed with preoccupied thoughts. "The truth is, I need quite a bit of help. But, most of them are personal, uh, confidential, sensitive or whatever the word is. I am not sure how to say. I mean, I need to be able to trust you before opening up everything to you. Sorry, was that too hurtful?"

"No, not at all. Please don't hesitate to speak your mind. I already told you. I am not here to take offense. I understand that I am a total stranger to you. I need you to feel absolutely comfortable before you disclose anything."

Lina nodded. She then asked, "What do you do for a living?"

"I work for a company called Milamek Corporation. My campus is in Rochester Hills. It's a Divisional office and I work in the Engineering department."

"Is it a big company?"

"Yeah. I think there are close to sixty thousand employees worldwide."

"Oh wow. Have you been with them for a long time?"

"Um, It's been around, what, four years and change. I was with another company for eight years; they were in Sterling Heights."

"So, lived in the Detroit area for a long time?"

"Well, for around twelve years, ever since I graduated from CTU."

"From where?"

"Cleveland Technological University in Cleveland."

"What did you study?"

"Uh, I did a Master's in Mechanical Engineering. Actually, two Master's, one of them only because the economy was in the dumps and I couldn't find a job."

"Do you live in Beniton Heights too?"

"Oh yeah or else I wouldn't have been able to reserve this

executive suite." Rakesh said with a smile as he swung his arm around the study room.

Rakesh continued, "Well, hang on a second."

Rakesh reached down into his pocket and pulled out his wallet. He usually kept few business cards stuffed among a collection of credit cards, reward cards, frequent flyer card, insurance card and his green card. More often than not, he carried more plastic than paper in his wallet, as he swiped for almost all purchases. He found two business cards, pulled one out, and handed to Lina.

"Here, I'll give you my card. That's my cell phone number which you already have. My office and the main campus numbers are right here." Rakesh pointed to the numbers on the business card. "You can call the main phone and ask to speak to Human Resources. You can inquire about me. I can let them know you'll call. I'll let my Manager know if you'd like to speak with him as well. Here, let me write down his name and office number."

Rakesh then turned the card and wrote his home address.

"This is the address where I live. It's a condo fancifully called Maple Valley Condominiums. It's on the corner of Rosemary and Maple Road."

"Thanks for doing this, Rakesh." Lina said as she took his business card. She looked at the card under his name. His job title listed him as a 'Senior Divisional Engineering Manager'.

"Wow, that's a mouthful of a lofty title," said Lina with a slight twist of her eyebrows and a grin. Rakesh shrugged his shoulders and laughed.

"Anyway," continued Lina, "I live just two miles from Hadley Lyons Elementary. Do you know where Ticonderoga Road is? The one off Macomb Line?"

"Yeah, I do."

"I live on Lamarr Avenue which is three streets down on Ticonderoga. We bought a house when we moved last summer to Beniton Heights."

"Uh-huh."

After a bout of reluctance, Lina said, "You know, uh, in the middle of everything going on, I think I missed the mortgage payment last month. I don't even know if I can afford the payments anymore. Anyway, uh, actually, I missed paying a whole bunch of bills. I got to tell you, those guys don't waste any time. Every one of them called me asking why I haven't paid up."

"Did you explain to them what happened?"

"Yes, I did. They pitied me and hung up after a friendly, but a stern reminder to pay up. Most of them offered to forgive the missed payment. 'Forgive' – that's the word they all used. But I bet, when I get the next statement, they wouldn't have forgotten to add interest and who knows, some penalty as well, for good measure."

Lina continued, "You see, Brian took care of paying all the bills and did whatever he did with both of our money. I didn't care. It wasn't my interest. I know we carry some debt besides the mortgage, but, uh, anyway, I've been trying to figure out what Brian did. I guess I've got to be able to pay the bills at least, before I figure out the rest."

"Would you like me to take a look at your bills and see if we both can sit down and sort them together?" Rakesh asked.

"I'd like that." Even as Lina answered immediately, she paused a while and hesitated before pursuing further. "Uh, but before we do, can I call your company and check to find out if you are, wait, let me see," Lina peeked at his business card and said, "Ahh, Senior Divisional Engineering Manager?"

"Absolutely, go for it." Rakesh chuckled.

After several more minutes chatting about nothing in particular, they left the study room, returned to the main lobby, and walked out the library. The building was connected to two other adjacent buildings, one of which had a café. Rakesh asked if she wanted to get a drink or a bite to eat, but she declined stating that she preferred to return home before Madeline woke up.

Then she asked, "Would it be alright if I call you on a weekday evening?"

"You can call me pretty much anytime. Remember, I am a veteran, uh, no, a lazy bachelor. I have plenty of free time. Just give me a call."

"Ok, will do." Lina replied with a smile.

In the parking lot, Lina thanked Rakesh and they both said their goodbyes. Rakesh once again offered a handshake. But, much to his surprise, Lina reached toward him and gave him a hug – a hug which seemed to betray her vulnerability and the enormity of her current situation, despite the courage and even humor that she displayed minutes earlier in the study room.

Rakesh clumsily hugged her back.

~~~   16   ~~~

At noon on Sunday, December 16th, Rakesh's phone rang. It was John Wharton.

"Hello, my friend." Rakesh chimed as he answered the call.

"You aren't still sleeping, are you?" John queried, knowing well Rakesh's weekend sleep-in habits.

"No, I am not. Can you believe I woke up almost three hours ago? I am just cleaning the house. What are you up to?"

"Nothing much. Look, if you are doing nothing for the rest of the day, why don't you come over? I'd like to chat about a few things."

"Yeah, sure. Give me about an hour or so and I'll be right there. Is something going on?"

"No, not at all. Just come over and we'll talk." John didn't say much.

Rakesh hung up and resumed his chores. Even without telling, he had a good conjecture of what John wished to chat about.

John Wharton took Karen's death hard. Considering the tragic circumstances of Karen Wharton's untimely death, Milamek Corporation generously offered John to stay off work for as long as he needed. John was grateful for the offer; consequently, he took time off to return his home back to order. He however soon discovered that the act of staying home depressed him more than staying at work. Everything he saw and touched reminded him of Karen. A many a times, he locked himself in the bathroom to relieve his grief in the form of sound sobs. In the end, he realized he had to distract himself away from memories of Karen. As a result, a few days after Karen's funeral, he returned to work and took deliberate efforts to remain as busy as he possibly could. Regardless, every sign of his grief was present – lurking just below his outer self.

His co-workers did not fail to notice either. John, a naturally inquisitive and a competitive person, not to mention cheerful, failed to display any of those traits. There were visible signs of his despondence. For one, for the better part of the work day, John chose seclusion over mingling. He kept his office door shut most times during the day and did not join his co-workers for lunch at the cafeteria, something he routinely did in the past. During meetings, he appeared to be lost in his own thoughts. Most of his colleagues assumed it to be normal and figured John would recover over time; therefore, allowed him the privacy he seemed to prefer.

Rakesh detected it as well, but as a close family friend, he couldn't simply ignore John. As a result, he made sure to walk into John's office on a regular basis to check on his state of mind. Rakesh engaged John in idle chat in an effort to distract him from his sense of loss. John's Manager and the company's Human Resources discussed counseling options for John; however, they too decided to allow more time as they presumed John was undergoing a normal grieving process rather than anything sinister.

Besides maintaining close contact at work, Rakesh visited John at his house, as he did before Karen's death. His visit seemed to encourage John to dissipate his sadness through private conversations with Rakesh. It also provided a sense of normalcy for the twins – a feeling of good old times. The most positive of all, amid the prevailing circumstance, was the fact that John enjoyed an abundance of family support.

One of the family members who offered unconditional and one-hundred percent support was Abigail Wharton. Abigail, John's aunt from his father's side was the youngest of the four siblings. Abigail went by both Abby and Gail, depending on what she allowed the other person to call her. She was widowed and lived off a lifelong annuity which her husband carefully planned and left for her. She was fifty-six years old, had no children, and resided in a modest three bedroom home in the suburbs of Louisville, Kentucky. Her house was paid off from the term life insurance money that she received following her husband's death. She also changed her last name back to her maiden name of Wharton. A healthy, vibrant, and an active person, Abigail kept herself busy with a variety of indoor and outdoor activities. Amid all that, she discovered she had few more free hours. In a determination not to waste those precious hours, she took up part time employment at a local bakery. While she displayed a sense of excellent customer service, the bakery sold delicious cakes, cookies, bread, pastries and hot beverages. Abigail did not require any more money than what she received from the annuity; however, she enjoyed the extra income off the bakery, which she titled 'play money'.

Abigail Wharton became the first to arrive in Detroit when the family heard about the details of the shooting on October 29th. She assumed the lead and took care of the twins, comforted John, notified other members of the family, and made all arrangements for Karen's memorial service and the funeral. She did not stop there. After the funeral, she flew back to Louisville, quit her bakery job, packed a couple of suitcases worth of clothes, locked her house, and drove to Beniton Heights to stay with John and the twins for as long as he needed.

No one appreciated more than John since he doubted he could handle everything by himself. Rakesh, for his part, during his visits to John's house, took an instant liking for this amicable woman who never seemed to rest a moment. The one thing Abigail was not familiar with was the city of Beniton Heights and the surrounding area. For this, she came to rely upon Rakesh as she wasn't sure if John was emotionally strong enough to keep up with Abigail's requests for errands. Rakesh never failed to oblige.

Abigail invited Rakesh for the Thanksgiving dinner in late November. Due to the closeness of time since Karen's death, the dinner was somber; nevertheless, Abigail tried her best to cheer everyone. They reminisced the prior Thanksgiving dinners that they had with Karen. On that night, as the group chatted, John Wharton broke the news to Rakesh. He decided to return to the Louisville area for good in order to stay closer to the family, particularly Abigail. Rakesh wasn't entirely surprised; John did not appear to cope well all by himself and for the most part, relied on Abigail.

Even so, Rakesh was quite taken aback at the relative quickness of John's decision, for it had been just less than a month since Karen's death. Since his continuingly evolving plan involved quitting Milamek Corporation, John requested that the discussion be kept confidential until he was certain beyond doubt that the plan would indeed come to fruition.

Another influencing factor driving John's decisions was Abigail herself, for, she initiated and proposed the idea of John's relocation. She in fact encouraged John to consider her suggestion seriously. Yes, her idea would necessitate the twins to attend a different school in the middle of the academic year; however, they were already in a different school now. Hadley Lyons Elementary still remained a crime scene and stayed closed. Students who attended Hadley Lyons were consequently transferred to other Beniton Heights elementary schools depending on how far the individual students lived from the other schools. Needless to say, this resulted in children who were in the same classroom to be scattered in different schools. Everyone considered this hastily put together action plan to be better than letting the children stay home for an indefinite period of time. The decision makers believed the current course of action would bring some sense of normalcy in the lives of the children, parents, teachers, and the staff alike.

John detailed his Louisville relocation plan to Rakesh. He would sell his house in Beniton Heights, move in with Abigail, and settle the twins into the new school after Christmas break. By living in her home, in the event he failed to sell the house quick enough, he wouldn't, at the least, be burdened with another mortgage in Louisville. Also, Abigail would shuttle the kids back and forth. John had high confidence his aunt would take care of the boys more than he ever could by himself. John couldn't have asked for more. The only thing remaining was for John to find employment in the Louisville area. Milamek Corporation did not have a presence in the Louisville area and even if they did, there were no guarantees the company would relocate John as they did a few years ago, especially on a short notice.

One week into December, John informed Rakesh that his interview with Brent & Cooper went extremely well and they were poised to make him an offer soon. Brent & Cooper, or B&C according to the inside folks, was a medical device manufacturer. The company equaled in size and bureaucracy to that of Milamek Corporation and had its global headquarters in Mississauga, Ontario – a major city encompassing the Greater Toronto Area. The Louisville campus positioned itself as one of B&C's primary facilities in the USA.

With these rapid evolution of plans in the life of John Wharton, Rakesh, on this Sunday afternoon of December 16th, had indeed a good conjecture of what John wished to chat about.

Rakesh arrived at John's home around two o'clock and was greeted by the twins and Abigail. John emerged from the other room and said hello to his friend. Abigail, as she always did, offered a choice of beverages and refused to take a no for an answer. Rakesh finally settled for some lemonade. John dismissed the twins, who clamored for Rakesh's attention, with the excuse that the two men had something very important to discuss.

"Rakesh, I am going to miss you a ton," began John.

"So, I take that you have received the offer from Brent & Cooper?" Rakesh did not find the need to guess too much.

"Yes, I did and I have accepted it as well. I had to get them to move fast since I told them I had to move to Louisville during the holidays."

"So, are you putting the house for sale?"

"Well, here is the deal. The new position is not open until February next year. It has something to do with the woman who's currently in this position. I think they promoted her and she's relocating to their German R&D location, somewhere in Munich. But, that's not happening until the middle of January. Anyway, they rushed and sent me the offer so I can work on my relocation plan."

"That's gracious of them." Rakesh was impressed at what a bureaucracy can achieve if they put their mind into the effort.

"Here is the best part. They offered to buy my house for the value they appraised. The good thing is I am getting the house sold with zero efforts. The flip side is I am not making any money out of it. But that's alright. I'd rather not be depressed living in this house which reminds me of Karen all the time. They are also paying for my relocation. So, all in all, it's not a bad deal at all."

"Hey, that's wonderful," said Rakesh. Then he asked, "When are you announcing your resignation?"

"Tomorrow. I'll get all of January for myself to get everything settled before starting at B&C."

"Are you planning on moving after Christmas or before?"

"I figured I'll move as soon as the school closes for the December break. Well, that's almost around the corner. Anyway, the boys will have at least a few days of holiday to settle down and prep up for the new school."

"Great idea. You know, you are right. I will miss you all a whole bunch. I am terribly sorry you are moving under such circumstances, but I wish you and the boys the best. Don't forget me and keep in touch," Rakesh said, truly saddened.

"Thanks Rakesh. Thanks for everything you have done for us, especially, thank you for taking care of the situation and the boys on the day Karen died."

"Anytime, my friend. Glad to be of help," replied Rakesh.

"Hey, guess what?" John bubbled. "Maybe, without me bugging you all the time, who knows, you might find someone and get married. You still have the collection of pictures of all the prospective brides your mom sent from India, don't you?"

Rakesh rolled his eyes and laughed. He then quipped, "Yeah, sure. That was the only thing I missed in my life. Anyway, as far as the pictures go, they haven't stopped. My parents have now managed to upgrade the technology in their lives. So, these days the photos arrive by email."

~~~   17   ~~~

The phone call from Lina came sooner than Rakesh expected. Rakesh recalled Lina asking him, just the past Saturday, if she could contact him on a weekday and Rakesh had replied yes. Around five on Monday evening, on December 17th, here it was. Rakesh at the moment was stuck in traffic on the congested sections of I-696 driving home from work. Usually, he did not leave until well after five. With the holiday right around the corner however, the pace of work had considerably slowed down allowing him to wrap up the day's chores and depart earlier. Yet, the traffic was already gathered on the freeways and snarled at the usual sections. Unlike the first time, Rakesh instantly recognized the caller and answered the call while moving at less than fifteen miles an hour.

"Lina Pratt. How are you?" Rakesh answered in a cheerful voice, enunciating her name with a purposeful exaggeration.

"I am fine. You?"

"Having a gala time on 696 with the crazy traffic all around me." He could hear Madeline over the phone. She sounded like any other normal hyperactive two year old.

"I can hear Madeline. Are you home?" Rakesh asked.

"Yes, I am. Is this a good time to talk?"

"Sure. What can I do for you?"

"Are you free the rest of the evening?"

"I guess so. I've got nothing going on. Why?"

"Would you be able to come over to my house? I'd like your help in going over few things. Remember the bills I talked about?"

"Yes, I do, and yes, I can come over. Do you need me to bring anything?"

"No, that's alright. Do you eat meat?"

Rakesh wondered what meat-eating had to do with the bills. "Yes, I do."

Lina said, "I am making pasta and meatballs. Will you have dinner with us?"

"Absolutely. What can be more delicious than pasta and meatballs?" Rakesh replied with a pleasantly surprised expression.

Lina laughed.

Rakesh remembered something. "I thought you wanted to verify my identity and be able to trust me. Are you sure you are okay with me coming over to your house?"

"Yeah, I am okay. By the way I already checked your background."

"You really did? That was fast. Did you speak with the HR?"

She replied, "Well, I spoke with Nathan Balcom. Do you remember him?"

"Nathan Ba…, oh my gosh, you mean Nate? How in the world do you know him?" Rakesh shook his head in sheer surprise. Nate Balcom was Rakesh's Manager at the firm he worked prior to joining Milamek Corporation.

"I don't," replied Lina. "Here is what happened. I thought I'd find someone who did not expect my call. I figured that would be a better way to check you out. So, I called the main number you gave me, spoke to your HR, who by the way, as you had mentioned on Saturday, was expecting my call. I asked her if she would be kind enough to tell me where you were employed before you worked at Milamek, and she did. I later called the outfit, spoke to someone, and told them I was from a prospective employer conducting a background check and needed to speak with your ex-Manager. They put me through Nathan's phone."

"Wow, interesting. So, what happened?" Rakesh's surprise remained unabated.

"Well, Nathan turned out to be helpful. I told him a bit about myself and the reasons behind my call and he was glad to help. He had nothing but wonderful things to say about you. Looks like you accomplished miracles at this company." Lina chuckled as she spoke of Nate's praises for Rakesh.

"I am truly amazed. Well, at least, Nate didn't bad-mouth me. I would have starved without the pasta tonight."

Lina laughed. "You aren't mad at me for lying about the background check, are you?"

"Well, if I may," Rakesh began with a sarcastic tone, "I am not entirely pleased at your conniving methods. But, if I can extend you the benefit of the doubt and put a positive spin, I must compliment you on your resourcefulness. What else did you do? Call the FBI?"

She laughed again and asked, "At what time do you think you'll be here?"

"Uh, it shouldn't take more than thirty minutes from where I am right now. I'll come straight to your house. Didn't you say you live on Lamarr?"

"Yes, I do. It's 568 Lamarr. Do you need directions?"

"Nope. I know where it is. I'll see you in a few minutes."

After they hung up, Rakesh continued driving toward Beniton Heights. The traffic situation improved ever so slightly allowing Rakesh to move at forty miles an hour on a freeway carrying a posted limit of seventy miles an hour. While he drove, he pondered how his newly formed acquaintance with Lina would forge over a long time.

Upon nearing Beniton Heights, Rakesh figured it might be a nice gesture to bring something for the toddler, Madeline. Hurriedly, he searched for an appropriate retail store on his phone and found a Target store inside a plaza off Macomb Line Road. After a rapid search of the aisles in what was uncharted territory for him, Rakesh bought a Princess Ariel Undersea Castle Lego building toy. Pleased at his shopping ability, he hurried back to his car and headed toward Lamarr.

A little after six, Rakesh parked his car by the curb, walked to the door, and rang the bell at Lina's two story colonial home. She opened the door, greeted and welcomed him in. Lina's home, located in an above-average subdivision, was one of over one hundred and fifty homes spread among a mix of six avenues, courts, circles, and crescents. The homes, less than eight years old, were part of the construction frenzy to meet the demands of the Beniton Heights' growing population. Most homes were constructed by a monopoly of one or two builders who bought the lots in bulk. In conforming to the local ordinance, the elevation of the homes projected sufficient difference in order to simulate randomness; in reality, however, each builder possessed no more than four floor plans which were mixed and matched to create further randomness. Most homes carried a two story colonial architecture with brick frontage, and brick and aluminum siding on the remaining three sides. Lina's home, a little over two thousand square foot building, had a foyer which opened to the second floor ceiling. The oak stairs to the second level lay on the right. To the left, on the corner, was the study. At the back of the house was the kitchen, breakfast area, and the family room. There was a formal dining room with entry from behind the stairs.

Rakesh removed his winter coat and shoes while he stood in the foyer. He said hello to Madeline who stood next to Lina with a shy smile and a tight grip on her mother's hands. Madeline waved her tiny hands back at him. He offered the Lego toy to her. Madeline let go of her mother's hand, approached him, took the toy with excited curiosity, and almost instantaneously retreated once again to her mother's side. Rakesh attempted few seconds of baby talk and Madeline responded with shyness. Eventually, she lost interest in Rakesh in favor of her new toy and walked away to another room to explore. For someone who lived with an active toddler, Lina kept her home well organized with the exception of a few stray items. Rakesh tended to stay organized as well, but only due to the fact he managed not to possess anything beyond what he absolutely needed. In other words, his home was organized by virtue of its bareness.

Following Lina to the kitchen area, he found one eight by ten frame holding the family picture. Brian Pratt held Madeline on his lap while Lina had her arms around Makenzie. This was the first time he saw the faces of the two lives lost along with Karen Wharton. Rakesh took a long and deep look at Brian and Makenzie. He was saddened by the brutal fact that the two now represented nothing more than a memory for Lina and Madeline. He was quite sure Madeline would, over time, lose her recollection of her father and big sister.

"This is the only picture I have kept," remarked Lina, as she noticed Rakesh looking at it. "I took the rest and put them in boxes," she sighed. "You know, I'd like to keep them and remember all the things we did together, but it is way too painful for me. I miss them a lot and besides, Madie keeps asking when dad is coming back. So, this one picture is sort of a compromise. Maybe I need to move out of this house. I don't know. There are way too many things to think about."

Rakesh felt the urge to put his arms around and hold her as she agonized over a multitude of things that were and weren't under her control. He hesitated instead, and stood there nodding in silence.

"C'mon in over here, please sit down." Lina motioned as she offered him a chair at the breakfast table.

"You have a beautiful home."

"Thanks, is there something I can offer to drink?"

Rakesh declined.

"Well, dinner is ready. Madie is usually hungry by now. I think her new toy is distracting her. Let me go check what she is up to. Are you hungry?"

Rakesh nodded yes.

A little later, the three sat down and ate dinner in relative silence.

After dinner, Rakesh lent a hand to clean the table and load the dishwasher. Madeline was distracted by her numerous play items, and once every few minutes, she brought a toy to Rakesh for a demonstration. By now, she shed her shyness and became comfortable enough to occasionally jump up on Rakesh's lap as she ran around the house. Rakesh had by now become proficient in dealing with small children after those few years with John Wharton's twins, Josh and Jake. This gave him the confidence to play along with the toddler quite competently. At one point, much to Lina's amusement, Madeline sat on Rakesh's lap, and with abundant curiosity toyed with his mustache.

Another hour passed before Madeline showed signs of slowing down for the evening. As the two adults chatted, she walked over to Rakesh and rested her head on his lap. Rakesh lifted her and wrapped his arms around her. Madeline snuggled and made herself comfortable on his lap. The sight of Madeline curled on Rakesh's lap flooded Lina's memories of Brian. She recalled the many times when Madeline cuddled with Brian as she dozed off. Madeline had the same curled posture now; only, it was not with her dad. Lina couldn't decipher if Madeline missed her dad or if she even comprehended anything. In any case, the scene in front of her stirred Lina's emotions enough to bring her to tears - enough for more than few to streak down her cheeks. Rakesh noticed and attempted to say something; however, Lina quickly stood up, walked over to the kitchen, and wiped her eyes.

A few minutes passed before Madeline fell asleep. Lina carried her to the upstairs bedroom to tuck her in for the night. With the adults now to themselves, Rakesh broke the brief silence. "Madeline is quite active, isn't she?"

"Oh yeah, she is. I think she was all the more excited to have someone else in the house besides her mom. Do you want some popcorn?"

"Sure, why not."

Lina returned with a container of freshly micro-waved, mild butter popcorn.

They nibbled on the popcorn for a minute or so in silence before Rakesh spoke first. "So, Lina, what did you have in mind that you wanted to talk about?"

"Well, I don't think I can afford this house anymore," she replied abruptly. "Also, I have a pile of bills which I need to pay and I am not sure if the pile is all that is due."

"Why do you say so?"

"Uh, I think Brian paid few bills online and I have no idea which ones. Anyway, I looked at the mortgage statement, and I think I've said this before, they've added the penalty for missing the payment last month even though they waived the payment. But, I can't afford these payments anymore."

"Ok, today is the seventeenth. When are these bills due? Did you check?"

"I think some of them are already late."

"Alright, let's do one thing at a time. Grab all the paper bills you have. Let's take a look and we'll write down if anything seems missing. Let's also talk about your mortgage, alright?"

"Okay. Let me get them."

Lina walked over to the study and returned with a stash of envelopes of different sizes. Rakesh removed all the bills from their envelopes and stacked them on the breakfast table. He then checked the due dates and made two piles – one that was past due and others that weren't, although, a few were very close to the payment due date. He also quizzed Lina on a long list of expenses common to any household and discovered at least six bills missing from the table. Lina suggested those could be the ones that Brian paid online. Rakesh then proceeded to jot down everything he had in front of him, and everything else they might be missing.

Rakesh asked the details of her bank balance and the means to access it. Lina appeared unaware and confirmed by admitting she didn't know how Brian managed the bank account. She remained unsure of the number of accounts they held. She did however mention her salary was deposited directly into the checking account which they had in the First Valley Bank. Rakesh continued to ask several additional questions and received at best, sketchy responses from Lina. He began wondering how he was going to sort this out for her. Eventually, Lina had a revelation. She mentioned Brian kept an electronic file somewhere in their home laptop. She suspected that the file might possess entire details of the financial records including login access to anything Brian may have done online. Rakesh certainly hoped that there was indeed something for him to dig through.

Lina returned with the laptop and fired it up. After several minutes of searching through the laptop, they found the file Lina referred to. Rakesh reviewed the contents and found the online access information for everything they needed for the moment. Relieved, he quickly explained to Lina what they were and she seemed to grasp it well. Rakesh suggested that they determine the balance in the account so they could first pay the past due bills before moving on to the ones which were due soon. Lina agreed. Rakesh helped her navigate through the online screens of her bank account and explained the various items that were displayed on the screen.

They discovered four accounts on the bank website. The two joint accounts were a checking and a savings account. The remaining two were credit card accounts issued by First Valley and linked to the same login credentials. Rakesh reviewed each of the accounts and showed Lina the details of the contents. There were outstanding amounts in both the credit cards. One of the credit cards showed a balance of $4852.36. Rakesh clicked the link to that account to investigate the details. Several miscellaneous charges showed up followed by a charge from the Hemmann Green Crematorium for an amount of $3675. This was one of the accounts Lina had failed to pay last month, and Rakesh noticed the late payment and finance charges tagged to the account.

As they browsed through, Rakesh noticed she had $1670 in the savings account while the checking account indicated, among other debits and credits, a recent salary deposit from Lina's employer. Rakesh proceeded to review the checking account for all the historical payments and tallied them with what lay on the breakfast table. He wanted to gather a complete picture of the financial transactions and understand how Brian handled them.

After spending a considerable time into what became a late night session at Lina's home, Rakesh finally had a decent grasp on what needed to be accomplished in terms of paying all the outstanding bills. He was relieved to know, at least so far, there were sufficient funds to pay all the bills, except her mortgage. He showed her how to pay most of those. The mortgage, which amounted to fifteen hundred dollars a month, required additional attention and needed to be dealt with at another time. In addition, for now, Lina would have to contend with just the minimum payments on her credit cards. At this point, Lina brought up two other expense accounts. One for Madeline's daycare which amounted to eight hundred dollars – the only bill Lina seemed to be in charge; and the other, a debt consolidation loan payment of three hundred dollars a month.

Armed with the knowledge of Lina's financial obligations, Rakesh made a mental calculation and compared the result with the direct deposit amount of her salary. He instantly realized Lina was right – she would no longer be able to afford her home. Nevertheless, he wanted to identify any possible means to increase the net amount of her salary. In the interest of helping her out, despite the sensitive nature of the question, he went ahead and asked, "Lina, how much do you earn?"

She told him. He earned close to three times what she did.

"Were you able to afford all the expenses with Brian's earnings?"

"Most of the time we did okay. Brian worked for different contractors all the time and his salary went up and down all the time. That's why we have this loan, because we had a bunch of credit card debts and Brian said something about consolidating them into one loan."

Rakesh was tempted to ask why in the world they decided to buy such an expensive home. However, he voted against it as there was no point debating the damage already done. In any case, he went there to help, not preach.

"Where did Brian work?"

"Oh, he was an electrician by trade. But he also worked on air conditioning stuff and knew a good bit of plumbing; enough to get steady work from various builders and contractors. We had some rough times when the recession hit, and two more years after that. But, after we moved to Beniton Heights, he stayed busy and received decent wages."

"Did he have any life insurance?"

"No."

"Are you sure?"

"Yes. That was something we talked about, considering his line of work, but I don't know, we never got one."

"Alright. Have you paid this month's daycare?"

"Yeah, I did. I took cash from the bank."

"Oh, you're right. That was the cash debit I saw on your account. Ok, very well. Now that, all other bills are taken care of, the only thing left for you to pay this month are your mortgage, cable and the water bill."

"Uh-huh."

"Here's the scoop. You have enough money to pay the cable and water, but not the mortgage. By the way, are you off from work the week of Christmas?"

"You mean next week? Yes, we are closed through New Year."

"Perfect." With the knowledge they had abundant time during the holiday, Rakesh came up with a tentative plan.

"Here is what we are going to do. We are going to spend the holiday week together to sort out a few things. Ok? First, we finish paying the rest of the bills for December. Then, we are going to figure out what you want to do with the house – sell, stay, move, whatever - and do just that as soon as the New Year begins. I am saying this because you are correct - you can't afford the mortgage payments anymore. Then, we are going to look at your savings and other financial accounts and sort them out. While we do that, we are going to figure out how to get you out of all the debts, starting with the four thousand and something dollars you owe on one of your credit cards. Finally, we'll make a plan on how you are going to deal with the finances and bills in the future, starting January. This means we'll have to look at what you can cut down and how. How are we doing so far?"

"Ok, I guess." Lina appeared substantially relieved upon hearing of a solid path of action from Rakesh. In the midst of all this, most of the popcorn remained untouched.

"Good. By the way, I am so glad you don't have any car payments."

"No, we don't. I am glad too. Brian was not into new cars and he drove that rusted piece of, uh, I mean that old Dodge truck. Mine runs well too. So, I am ok for now."

"Alright, hang on a second. I am going to my car to grab my backpack. I'll be back."

"Ok." Even as she answered, Lina had a perplexed expression as to why Rakesh needed the backpack.

When he returned, Rakesh reached in and pulled out his checkbook. He always kept one or two booklets of check leaves in his backpack. Lina looked at him questioningly. "What are you doing?"

"I am writing a check for your December mortgage payment. It is due Thursday. So, don't forget to drop it off in the mailbox tomorrow." Rakesh said, as he filled out the check and tore it off the booklet.

This was altogether unexpected. Surprised and stunned, Lina hastily protested. "Rakesh, you don't have to do this. I can't accept it."

"I know I don't have to do anything. But I am going to."

"But, you don't understand. I can't afford to pay you back and I don't want to be stuck in an obligation."

"I understand. But let me clear up a few things. This check is not a loan and is certainly not a charity. I committed to help you and I am not going back on my words. You don't have to pay me back and more importantly, you absolutely do not owe me any favors or obligations whatsoever, do you understand?"

"But, what happens next month? I can't keep expecting to be bailed out like this, can I?" She felt both grateful and embarrassed by Rakesh's check and Rakesh seemed to take note of her state of mind.

"Well, that is why we are going to talk over the holidays about what happens next month and beyond. Lina, I am not bailing you out. What I mean is that I want to make sure we put something together so you can live within your means. That's going to take some time and I am just acting as a bridge until then. Please don't think I am here to embarrass you. That is definitely not my intent."

"No, what you are doing means a lot to me. I just don't want to become dependent on your money. Besides, what happens if you yourself get in a bind writing me checks? I mean, the mortgage payment is not a small amount."

"First of all, I promise you are not going to become dependent. I might offer to fix few things now and then, but only until sometime - until you get into a stable routine. Also, I've never in my life spent money on someone else. So, without going into too much detail, let's just say, I'll be ok to an extent. Anyway, we'll talk more some other time."

It was clear to Lina that Rakesh wasn't about to budge. As a result, she accepted the check.

When everything was said and done, Rakesh looked at the clock. It showed eleven forty pm. He checked his calendar on his phone for any meetings that may be scheduled for Tuesday, and to his relief, found none. All the meetings stood cancelled as many employees were already on vacation.

On his way out, Lina thanked him profusely for sorting out her biggest headache of the month. Of course, there was more to deal with, but she was immensely relieved that Rakesh had promised to work with her to sort them all out. Rakesh thanked her for the dinner and asked her to call him if she needed anything. They then parted for the night with an embrace which was much warmer and lasted longer than the one, two days ago.

~~~   18   ~~~

The remainder of the week passed by with nothing of significance occurring, as both Lina and Rakesh kept to their respective routines and chores. The only exception happened to be the phone calls between them - three days in a row following his visit to her home. The reasons for the telephone conversation varied, but stayed focused on the most pressing issue lingering right now – the timely payment of bills. She either had questions to ask, or wanted to notify him that she mailed the necessary payments. In any event, the reasons served as an opportunity for them to chat with each other. The calls were short, but Rakesh savored the conversations with her while he took care to preserve a semi-professional candor. From his quite a brief acquaintance – less than a week - Rakesh detected Lina to be an interesting paradox. She appeared resourceful in many ways, but also seemed to struggle or remain naive on others. She was by all means a smart individual, and Rakesh assumed her reasons for naivety to be more due to her disinterest or indifference regarding certain things. During their conversation, she fluxed between confidence and vulnerability. Despite the display of her witty and carefree traits at most times, she also turned around and became defensive at other times. For Lina however, the conversations with Rakesh so far served as a good distraction from her continued depressed state of mind. In addition, she found Rakesh to be a fair and reasonable sounding board to vent her thoughts.

In the meantime, in addition to their usual chat at the office, Rakesh and John Wharton spoke a few times over the phone. By the end of the week, John seemed quite a bit at peace despite the hurt over the loss of his wife. He had plenty of reason to be relaxed since he had given his resignation and looked forward to his move to Kentucky. The movers contracted by John's new employer, Brent & Cooper, were scheduled to arrive just after Christmas. The moving company had the responsibility for both packing and unpacking their belongings, and to relocate their personal vehicles. This left John with not much to do in preparation for the relocation. On the same week, Brent & Cooper was taking possession of his home. John and his aunt Abigail completed all the arrangements to enroll the twins, Josh and Jake, in their new school. With paperwork signed and all tasks accomplished, John, of course, had every reason to be relaxed. The plan entailed handing over the keys to the relocation contractors and depart Beniton Heights with Abigail on Sunday, December 23rd.

On Friday the 21st of December, Milamek Corporation resembled a ghost town. A significant number of employees were off on vacation. On this last day of work for the year, those who were at work were not working. Around ten in the morning, Rakesh entered the cafeteria and observed John bidding farewell to his co-workers. A few minutes later, John walked over to Rakesh and sat across him on one of the cafe chairs.

"Is anything going on for you tomorrow?" John asked.

"Uh, I am meeting with an acquaintance of mine in the afternoon. It might drag into the evening, although I am not sure as of now." Rakesh's response was in reference to his plans on spending time with Lina to go over a few things that they had discussed previously during the week. Once again, Lina had asked if he would have dinner with her and Madeline.

"Acquaintance? What sort of word is that? Are you into some kind of a business meeting?"

"No, it's a new friend I happened to know."

A sense of elevated curiosity and excitement hit John. "Jeez man, you sound scandalous. Is it a girl?"

"Sorry to disappoint you, my friend. There is nothing scandalous. And let me see. A girl? Well, if you must know, yes it's a woman."

Wide eyed, John had an expression of amazement. "Holy shit! Finally, the bachelor is turning around, I see."

Evidently uncomfortable, Rakesh squirmed in his cafeteria chair. Nevertheless, he was amused and glad to hear the free spirited voice of John which had been missing lately. "Stop! There's nothing going on. I just know her since last week and I am helping her with few things. So, grow up and quit taunting me."

John wasn't about to quit. "Helping her out? Is this what they call these days? Oh man, this is sweet. Is she one of your mom's email photo bride?"

Rakesh laughed loud and then quipped in a sarcastic tone. "Yeah, sure, if you can imagine my mom – a traditional Indian lady - sending pictures of white, Caucasian American women."

"Well, well, well. A white girl for the Indian, huh? This is scandalous, after all. Who is she?"

In an urge to halt the childish conversation which was occurring at Lina's expense, Rakesh became serious and said, "John, that's enough. I am not involved with anyone. Plus, it's far more serious. Her name is Lina. Her husband and daughter were killed in the Hadley Lyons school shooting."

John's expression changed to one of shock. He looked stunned. Then he blurted out, "I am so sorry Rakesh. I didn't mean to make light of the situation. Goddamn!"

"That's alright. Don't beat yourself up. They…"

John interrupted Rakesh with a startling recollection of the various news and investigative reports he had read and heard about. "Christ! Her husband and daughter, uh, are they the two who were in the classroom with Karen in the parent-teacher meeting?"

"Yes, that's right."

"Oh my gosh! Shit! That's terrible. How is this woman holding up?"

"Well, considering what a mess she was on the day of the shooting, she is a lot better now. She has another daughter, a two year old, that she has to care for. So, I am thinking, that's keeping her distracted."

"She has another daughter? How old is she?" John sounded surprised.

"I just told you, two years old."

"No, damn it. How old is this woman, uh, Lina?"

"I have no idea. I never asked. She looks quite young, though."

"How did you get to know her?"

Rakesh, in as much brevity he could muster, explained the circumstances of how he came across Lina at the recycling shed on the day of the shooting and how they later met. Since he had promised Lina utmost confidentiality of all conversations between him and her, he did not elaborate any further. Fortunately, John did not press for details either.

A moment of silence passed as John appeared to be lost in thought. "Anyway, do you think you can make it to my house for dinner tomorrow?"

"I think so. You are driving to Louisville on Sunday, aren't you?"

"Yeah, we are. The boys have been asking for you."

"You know what, I'll come over. Lina and I should be able to wrap up before five and I'll be at your place after that."

"Perfect. That should work. Hey, wait a minute. Why don't you bring her along for dinner?"

"Who? Lina?"

"Yeah, who else?"

"Uh, I am not sure if she would be ok with that." There was hesitance in Rakesh's voice, as he replied.

"C'mon, ask her. We'd be thrilled to have her and her little one. It will be a nice get together. Will you ask her? I promise I'll behave myself."

"Alright, I'll ask."

"Wonderful. I am looking forward. My dear Aunt and the boys would be excited. Well, I should get back to my office. I'll talk to you later."

After work, Rakesh spoke to Lina over the phone, brought up the conversation he had with John earlier that day, and inquired if she would be interested in joining him for dinner at John's house on Saturday. Upon hearing his query, Lina instantly recalled her connection with the Wharton family – a connection in which the tragic event of October 29th stemmed as the only common denominator. Therefore, Lina's reluctance was understandable. "I am not sure Rakesh. Wouldn't it be awkward, me being there?"

Realizing her discomfort, Rakesh made an attempt to assuage her concerns. "Well, it's entirely up to you whether or not you want to go. If you think you'll be uncomfortable, you may skip. But, knowing John, Abby, and the twins, they are a great company to be with. They are excited to have you and Madeline over. So, let me know and we'll decide from there."

After a short pause of what seemed to be a moment of pondering, Lina consented. "I guess, I'll be alright. I'll go."

"Excellent," said Rakesh.

On Saturday, Rakesh enjoyed his usual sleep-in until around eleven o'clock. For lunch, he heated up a random choice of frozen food selection off his freezer, and arrived at Lina's house after one pm. Rakesh did his best and continued to play the role of the money man. He attempted to sort out few more financial items that they both, earlier in the week, had agreed to work on. However, in the midst of all the serious conversation, both digressed from the topic of focus an ample number of times, thereby ending up in idle chat. Both exhibited subtle curiosity regarding each other's life, yet they held back under the cautionary premise of not been acquainted for long enough time.

While Rakesh remained determined to stay the course of a

professional discourse that he had committed to her, Lina appeared determined not to trap herself into a state of dependency on someone who was still a stranger, not to mention the fact that she held just a bit more than a rudimentary sense of trust for him. Despite their determination and reluctance, they enjoyed each other's conversation. In the end, the entire afternoon passed without accomplishing much.

At John Wharton's house, Lina had a delightful evening while Madeline was thrilled to play with the twins, who in turn awkwardly attempted to entertain her. Nevertheless, the boys enjoyed the company of an opposite gender who was by all means simply adorable. By the end of the evening, Madeline became adept at impersonating the war games the boys typically enjoyed.

As far as Abigail, true to her personality, she never failed to be a charm and she made a marked impression on Lina. Lina had forgotten what it was to be loved and cared for by a family member, and Abigail brought those memories back from what seemed to be a distant past. However, what differed from the past was the conspicuous absence of superficiality. In the end, Abigail's unadulterated and no-nonsense sense of caring helped elevate her stature in Lina's mind.

At almost ten in the night, Rakesh dropped Lina and Madeline back at their home. Fed with ample stimulation, from all the horseplay with the twins, Madeline had not fallen asleep as she usually did at this time of the hour. Before Lina stepped out of the vehicle, Rakesh invited her to visit him at his condo. Lina accepted his invitation and they decided to decide later as to when she might be able to come over. Rakesh helped Madeline out of her child seat and assisted in securing the car seat back into Lina's vehicle. Handling the car seat was one of the few things Rakesh learned during the years when he occasionally took care of John and Karen's twins. Today, he was grateful for the ability that saved him from something which could have easily become a humorously unwieldy task.

~~~   19   ~~~

The Christmas holiday was upon the populace. Lina and Rakesh were off from work for the next nine days. On Sunday morning, the day before Christmas Eve, Rakesh was inspired to pay a visit to big box retailers, the ones with children's products. He wasn't sure what he wanted to do or buy, but had the urge to get something for Madeline for Christmas. Letting his thoughts wander, he also realized, for whatever unknown reason, he had never bought anything for John's twins which could be strictly categorized as a toy. Somehow, bringing in a pizza or taking the boys out for a hot dog seemed easier than finding a toy.

Thumbing through the map on his phone, Rakesh found a Babies R' Us Store across the mall. An hour later, he was inside the store wandering and aimlessly gazing at all the toys the industry catered for boys and girls. There seemed to be more of pinks than blues, which in this case, worked in his favor as he was after all seeking something for Madeline. Sauntering through the aisles, he remembered the past Monday when Madeline had fallen asleep on his lap while he was at Lina's house. He wondered if the little child missed her father. He also wondered how Madeline perceived him. Perhaps, she was too young to compartmentalize such thoughts. He wasn't sure if the toddler was attached more to her father or mother, and how that might impact her as she grew up, assuming an impact existed at all in the first place.

Rakesh stopped at the section of shelves filled with baby carriers, strollers, child seats, and boosters. He decided he would buy a child seat for his car. He figured the seat might come handy if Madeline rode with him in his car. He wasn't sure why or how frequently Madeline might be riding in his car, but he bought one anyway, just in case. Motivated by his new purchase, he ambled over to the toy section and picked more than a dozen toys of all types. For good measure, he also selected a few crayons and miscellaneous craft material – the ones appropriate for a two to three year old. He contemplated purchasing a couple of sets of clothing; however, gave up after browsing through a dizzying array of clothes which didn't seem to make any sense. Clearly, he needed more experience before he could venture into clothing. Content that Madeline would have something to play with when she and her mom visited him at his condo during the holiday, he paid for his loot and drove home satisfied.

Lina visited Rakesh at his condo for the first time on Christmas Eve. When she and Madeline walked in, Rakesh picked up the toddler who was more than delighted to snuggle in his arms. The first thing Lina noticed was the predominantly bare home; nevertheless, everything was in its place. The basement had a finished room which appeared untouched or unused. As they walked up the stairs to the second level, she found a couch and a recliner in the living room. A flat screen TV sat in between the two box windows which were covered by simple drapery. At the breakfast area, under the low hanging chandelier was a modest rectangular breakfast table with a seating capacity of four. Five or six decorative pieces of art hung on the wall whose paint remained unchanged since the construction of the domicile. At the corner of the half wall that separated the kitchen and the living room area were the dozen or so toys which Rakesh had bought the previous day. They were unopened from their packaging. The bulky box which held the child seat lay next to the pile of toys.

"Expecting a child in the family, are you?" Lina remarked with amusement and pleasant surprise at the collection.

"Yeah, this little one." Rakesh pointed to Madeline who was still in his arms and eyeing the collection of toys. "These are all hers. Merry Christmas!"

"Why did you buy all these? She has all sorts of toys already. Thank you though. Wow, did you buy a car seat?"

"Well, let's just say, it'll come handy."

Lina looked at him and simply smiled.

Rakesh removed the toys from its packaging for Madeline to play with, as they continued to chat. A few moments later, with Madeline distracted with several play items, the two adults were left to themselves.

"I've ordered pizza for dinner. It should be here in a few minutes. Does Madeline need anything I need to get?" Rakesh was unprepared to host a small child.

"No, I brought everything she needs. She'll eat pizza. So, we're good to go. Do you cook at all?"

"Of course, I do. I pick out a random frozen food packet from the freezer, toss in the microwave for a few minutes, and off I go."

Lina glanced at him, shook her head, and laughed. "Let me see your fridge. May I?"

"Sure, knock yourself out. I am not sure if you can figure out what they all are."

Lina walked over to the kitchen, looked around, opened the fridge, peered inside, found a bottle of hot chilli pickle, picked it up curiously, and asked, "What is this?"

"That's Indian pickle. Not the wimpy dill pickles. These are quite hot. Would you like to try?"

"Hmm. It appears strange. What's in this thing?"

"Cayenne pepper, spices, and what not, all ground into a paste. Here, try some." Rakesh scooped a bit from the bottle with a spoon and handed to Lina. She sniffed the chunk and hesitated. "This smells spicy. Are these safe to eat?"

"Of course it is safe to eat unless you are allergic to spicy stuff. My life depends on this kind of food."

Lina tried. "Oh my god!" She exclaimed. "This is fuc.., uh, hot. How do you eat this, anyway?"

Rakesh laughed and proceeded to clarify. "Definitely not the way I gave you. This is not peanut butter to scoop up a spoonful. You eat pickles as a side relish or a dip to help improve the flavor of the main course." He continued, laughing, "Here, grab a spoon of yogurt; should help clear up the heat."

With yogurt in her mouth, Lina opened and peered in the freezer, only to find several food items, none of which she could recognize. She picked a few of them and queried Rakesh. He patiently explained what each of them was and how they were to be eaten and with what, and so on. In the meantime, the pizza arrived. While Lina and Rakesh sat down on the couch to eat, Madeline was content on settling on the floor with a plate of cut up pizza. After dinner, Rakesh tossed the meager number of cups and silverware into the dishwasher that already held a few more unwashed dishes.

Soon enough, Madeline was spent for the evening. With droopy eyes, she ambled over to Rakesh, and just as she did a few days ago, cuddled on his lap. A few minutes later, she fell asleep.

"Does she miss her dad?" Rakesh sensed a pattern in Madeline's behavior.

"Well, she was close to Brian. I can't completely figure out if she misses him, although she does ask for him once in a while," replied Lina.

"This cuddling thing she did with you," continued Lina, pointing to Madeline, "is what she always did with Brian as soon as she was sleepy or tired."

Rakesh nodded and went upstairs to return with a blanket and a pillow. As Lina watched, he put Madeline on the couch, covered her with the blanket, and dimmed the lights in the room. With the house quiet, within few minutes, the conversation inevitably returned to the more immediate pressing issues, beginning with Lina's home. After a brief discussion, Rakesh asked the primary question lingering in their minds. "Lina, do you want to live in the house you are living now?"

"No." Lina replied assertively. "Everywhere I turn, there are memories I can't handle. I'd be better off moving elsewhere."

"Elsewhere? Are you thinking of moving out of Detroit area?"

"No, no. I am saying I want to move out of my house. That's all. I have no reason to go anywhere else. It won't make a difference. I don't know anyone anyway, well, except for you now."

Rakesh turned his eyes toward her. He became increasingly curious regarding her assertion of not knowing anyone. He instead shelved his curiosity for another time and reverted to focus on the topic. "Well, then, I can come up with three options."

"Ok." Lina responded with elevated expectation.

"You can buy another house, something you can afford. You'll be in your own home, but also will carry a long term mortgage commitment. The next option is to move into an apartment. Obviously, you won't be in any long term commitment, but you wouldn't get to enjoy the so called perks of home ownership either."

Lina listened to him in silence.

He continued, "The last option is, you and Madeline can live in my home."

Lina had a startled expression. "Live with you? What does that supposed to mean?"

"I didn't say, 'live with me'. I said, 'live in this house'. There's a difference."

"Really, how so?"

"Alright, calm down," said Rakesh in his usual calm and assuring voice. "We are discussing options. That means they are just that – options. You can choose to accept or decline. So, can we simply discuss without bringing emotions in?"

"But, uh…" Lina began protesting.

"It's just a discussion. Can or can't we?"

She sighed. In a resigned tone, she asked, "So, what do you have in mind?"

"We were talking about the third option. If you both live in this house, you have no commitments, and no mortgage or rent to pay. The offer comes with free utilities as well. You don't need to sign any contract or deal. That frees you to pay for Madeline's daycare, your outstanding loan, and save some for yourself. I have two additional bedrooms, one for each of you. At any point of time, if you don't like the arrangement, you are free to leave with absolutely no catch."

Lina sat without uttering a word. Rakesh went upstairs to check on something and left her to mull over. When he returned, Lina asked, "Do you have any other options?"

"No, I don't. Do you?"

"Not really," admitted Lina.

More silence ensued.

"So, regarding your offer of the third option - to move into your home – do you think it's just that simple?" Lina asked.

"Why wouldn't it be? I spelled out the offer and I have also given you a way out if things don't work out as expected. Do these things need to be complicated to sound and feel important?"

"It wouldn't be appropriate, uh, you know, me moving in here."

"In whose opinion wouldn't it be appropriate?"

"I don't know. Your friends and other people might have something to say."

"My friends are not supporting and paying for my living, are they? I am sure they'll have a few comments, I am not denying. But, everyone is entitled to their opinions as long as they don't intrude. As far as other people, who might they be?"

"I don't know Rakesh. I am confused. You make it all sound as if it is not a big deal." She sounded frustrated.

"I am doing nothing more than trying to keep things simple as much as possible. Why don't we back up a bit and break it down into few baby steps, alright? You might then find them simple enough to handle. Let's start off by putting your house for sale as soon as the New Year rolls in. You have time to think over all the three options until your house sells."

"I told you before. I don't want to become dependent on you or your money. That's what living in your house will do, and besides, who does such things anyway? Simply moving in with someone on a whim?"

"Then you reserve the right to decline that option. You do have two other options, right? Listen, all I am asking you is to think over all the three possibilities before deciding on one. That's all. If you come up with any other options, let's talk about them. Fair enough?"

She looked at him briefly and looked away, but did not respond.

~~~   20   ~~~

After Lina left Rakesh's condo the previous night, she remained confused, conflicted, and on the defensive. Rakesh's offer to move into his house came as a complete surprise. What startled her more was the casual and arbitrary demeanor projected by Rakesh when he presented her with the perceivably controversial option. But then, the handwritten note she received from him at the funeral was casual and arbitrary as well. Nevertheless, the offer was quite tempting from a financial perspective, despite a significant number of ominous unknowns. What if Rakesh's offer was nothing more than lucrative bait which might turn sinister in the near future? What if he harmed Madeline? What if she became entangled in an unaffordable web of liability issues as a result of the co-habitation? Several 'what ifs' lurked with no answers. After agonizing over many possible combinations of doomsday scenarios, Lina eventually relaxed. For one, she figured she indeed had ample time to contemplate Rakesh's options. In addition, she failed, so far, to discern any malicious intent on Rakesh's part, despite the brevity of time they've known each other. In any event, she decided to keep all options for future housing open until her home sold.

The other disconcerting factor for her was the strong possibility of the erosion of her financial independence. Rakesh had already paid one of her outstanding mortgage payments. Later, during one of their frequent conversations, Rakesh nonchalantly mentioned that he would be willing to pay her mortgage bill until her house sold. He seemed genuine, unpretentious, and non-manipulative; however, she remained unsure if he made his offer in a heartfelt manner or bore any undesirable ulterior motive which could lead to something perilous. Consequently, she vehemently protested at his offer of mortgage payment. Rakesh patiently listened to her protests and inquired what her solution was in regards to paying the now unaffordable mortgage. She had none except for a foreclosure, bankruptcy or use of credit cards - all of which Rakesh refused to allow her to consider. He warned her of the detrimental consequences of considering such options. In the end, she wondered what tangible benefit Rakesh derived by remaining in her company and doing all the things he was doing for her. After all, she thought, he was a happy bachelor who lived a relatively carefree life. Now, for no particular reason, he chose to burden himself with her and the young child, along with the circumstances she was intertwined. Lina was also weighed down with the apprehension that Rakesh was being overly magnanimous, and he might be jeopardizing his own financial situation. She queried him a few times in an attempt to allay her own concerns, but he refused to tread into any details other than words of reassurance. In the end, Lina decided it would be in her best interest to get to know him further and attempt to establish a higher level of trust.

On Christmas day, Lina called Rakesh around eight thirty in the morning. Rakesh answered the phone in a drowsy voice, betraying his current state. He had not yet divulged the secret of his sleep-in to her.

"I am sorry, are you still sleeping?"

"Uh, yeah. That's alright. What's up?"

"We're coming to your house. May we?"

"Absolutely. Are you ok?"

"Uh-huh. I don't want to spend Christmas in my house. I just want to get out and most places are closed. So…"

"No, you're fine, come on over. Just bring a few things Madeline would need to eat. My kitchen is not yet child friendly."

The trio spent the Christmas day at Rakesh's condo without much fanfare. When Lina and Madeline arrived, the time was little after ten in the morning. Lina hadn't had breakfast; neither did Rakesh, and they were soon reminded of that fact by virtue of their growling stomach. Having had witnessed an array of frozen cuisine the last time she visited his house, Lina decided to take the reins and identify what they would have for brunch. She scouted the kitchen and the fridge and found a dozen eggs, half a loaf of bread, and five sprouting potatoes. After rustling through the cabinets and drawers, and along with Rakesh's aid, she found the necessary kitchenware to prepare the food. She skillet-fried the potatoes, made a few omelets, and toasted slices of the bread.

While she prepared the brunch, Rakesh invented games for Madeline; they both relished the time together as they concocted every conceivable silly act. Soon after, they ate a simple but sumptuous brunch. Rakesh was glad he had the inventory of appropriate food supply and was grateful for Lina's preparation of a hot meal.

They spent the rest of the day idling on the couch, watching a couple of movies, and playing with Madeline. In the evening, as they were chatting, Rakesh asked, "Do you want to go to Canada tomorrow for Boxing Day?"

"What's Boxing Day?"

"Well, as far as I know, it's the day after Christmas and is a national holiday in Canada, Britain, and Ireland. There might be few other countries which observe Boxing Day, but I am not sure. Since Canada is the closest of all, I thought I'd suggest going there."

Lina laughed. "That's it? It's a holiday? So, what's with the boxing?"

"Well, I think there are several stories. The one I've heard has to do with the servants of wealthy families who received boxes with gifts, bonuses, or food as gratitude for their service through the year. Anyway, today it's more like the Black Friday in the US. It's more of a shopping day, sale, and so on. Have you been to Canada?"

"No. Have you?"

"Yeah, a few times on business trips. Do you want to go?"

"I suppose. Where would we go in Canada?"

"It depends. If Madeline is game for a four plus hour drive, we can go to Toronto, spend time at the Eaton Centre - the biggest mall in downtown Toronto. It's a beautiful place. We could also wander the streets of Toronto which is a beautiful city, but it would be cold. If you are not in the mood for a mall, we could visit the CN tower and do what every tourist does. If you just want to check off the 'been there, done that' list, we could go to Windsor, right across the river from Detroit, visit the Devonshire mall and come back. That'll still qualify as a trip to Canada. What do you think?"

"If we go to Toronto, wouldn't we be late coming back?"

"No, we'll stay overnight near Toronto in a hotel and drive back Thursday."

"Hotel? No! I don't want to do that." Lina responded rather abruptly.

"You don't need to get all jumpy. You will have your own room with Madeline. Now, would that work?"

"No, I didn't mean…" Lina trailed off.

Rakesh looked toward her and reassured her. "Lina, I'd like to believe I am a reasonably decent person. I won't do anything to cause you or Madeline any embarrassment or harm. I do understand your need to build trust at your own pace and I get that, but I promise you no harm whatsoever. Do you understand?"

Lina quietly nodded.

"So, what do you say? Toronto or Windsor?"

"Let's go to Toronto. Madie should be ok. I'll get all the stuff she needs."

"Great. Don't forget to bring the stroller and her birth certificate. Do you have a passport?"

"Yes, I do. I think it's still valid. I'll check. Do you need to book the hotel rooms?"

"That won't be necessary. We'll just wing it. Several Holiday Inns are scattered along our route. We'll pick one along the way. I'll come and pick you both up tomorrow morning."

The next morning, they drove to the international border which was about forty minutes from Beniton Heights. Rakesh chose the Ambassador Bridge crossing. The bridge, a single span construction across the Detroit River, connected Detroit and the west side of the city of Windsor in Ontario. This was one of three international border crossings which connected Southwestern Ontario and metropolitan Detroit region. The other two crossing points were via the Detroit-Windsor tunnel and the Blue Water Bridge. The tunnel connected the downtowns of Detroit and Windsor and was an underwater highway across the Detroit River. The Blue Water Bridge was a two span construction across the St. Clair River and connected the cities of Port Huron in Michigan and Sarnia in Ontario.

They arrived at the toll booth at the entrance of the bridge via the newly renovated sections of the freeway and its exit ramps. Rakesh paid the toll, drove across the Ambassador Bridge, and lined up behind one of many vehicles waiting to pass through the Canadian immigration inspection.

Their turn came after a twenty minute wait. Rakesh pulled his vehicle to the booth window and greeted the officer of the Canada Border Services Agency or CBSA for short. The male officer said both 'Hello' and 'Bonjour' - they happened to be in one of the bilingual lanes. Rakesh replied back in English and offered all the documents to the officer. Scrutinizing Rakesh's green card, Lina's US passport, and Madeline's birth certificate, he began the series of routine questions.

"What are your citizenships?"

"Mine's India, they both are US citizens." Rakesh replied on behalf of everyone.

"Where do you all live?"

"Beniton Heights, Michigan."

"Where are you headed to?"

"Toronto."

"Why?"

"Just to visit the city, the Eaton Centre, and maybe the CN tower."

"How long will you be in Canada?"

"We're returning tomorrow evening."

"Any alcohol, tobacco, firearms or weapons in the vehicle?"

"No."

"Food or food products?"

"We have some snacks and some stuff for the child."

"Any gifts or purchased items staying in Canada?"

"No."

"What else are you bringing into Canada?"

"Nothing but our bags with clothes for the overnight stay."

"Is the child yours, hers or both of yours'?"

"She is her daughter."

"How are you related to the lady in the passenger seat?"

"She is a friend of mine."

"What is the name of the child's father?" The officer asked the question as he read Madeline's birth certificate.

"Brian Pratt." This time, Lina answered even as she wondered why the officer had to ask, despite Brian's name being available on the birth certificate.

"Why is he not accompanying you?"

"He is dead." Lina blurted out a bit too hastily.

Rakesh quickly intervened. "She lost her husband in the school shooting around two months ago."

The officer had a visible change in his expression. After a pause, he looked straight at Lina and said, "I am truly sorry about that. Is that the one at the elementary school?"

Lina nodded.

"Ma'am, are you and, let's see, Madeline? Yeah. Are you both traveling on your own free will?"

"Yes, we are," replied Lina.

The officer then swiped Rakesh's Green card and Lina's Passport on his computer scanner and stared at the computer display for a few seconds. Apparently satisfied at the lack of any negative background information, he turned toward them, returned the documents and said, "Okay. Here you go. Enjoy your trip."

After they stowed the documents where they belonged, Rakesh drove off and merged on Huron Church Road joining the abundance of tractor-trailers heading south toward highway 401. The sheer number of trucks was a testament to the fact that the bridge served as the busiest international crossing in North America in terms of trade volume.

As Rakesh maneuvered the lanes to pass the lumbering trucks on Huron Church, Lina asked, "Wow, is that pretty normal?"

"What is?" Rakesh asked.

"The bunch of questions at the immigration. Do they ask such personal questions?"

"Yes, they do. The important thing is to remain professional and answer to the point. Anyway, wait till you get to the US border on the way back. Usually, they tend to be stricter than the guys at the Canadian border."

What's with the 'am I travelling on free will' question?" Lina still remained intrigued with the experience of the border crossing.

"Well, they just want to make sure you are not being abducted or forced to ride with me. These things are a sort of behavioral and probing questions to determine if everything is okay or not."

"How come the officer didn't ask for your passport?" Lina asked.

"Because, my green card is sufficient to enter Canada."

"So… you are not an American?"

"You're right. I am a – in technical jargon – a lawful permanent resident. Anyway, I'll be eligible to apply for US citizenship soon."

"Well, I thought you were an American. You behave like one anyway."

"Which is how?"

"I don't know. Never mind. Have you lived in the States for long?"

"Oh gosh, yes. This is home for me for all practical purposes. Let's see, I've lived almost half of my life in the US."

"Where'd you live the other half?"

"In India."

"Were you born in India?"

"Yes."

A few minutes later, they were on highway 401 heading toward Toronto. Rakesh set his cruise control at one hundred and fifteen kilometers per hour where the posted limit was one hundred. He was aware of the unwritten rule where the traffic violation generally triggered at or above one hundred and twenty kilometers per hour. Even at their current speed, they noticed a number of vehicles passing them effortlessly; things would only get worse as they got closer to the Greater Toronto Area.

"Oh my goodness!" Lina exclaimed. "Look at all those wind turbines." She pointed toward the numerous turbines which stood tall on the flat farmlands on either side of the freeway. In the recent years, hundreds of wind turbines had mushroomed on the farmlands along highway 401. Few were right at the edge of the farms next to the freeway. The sheer size of those three blades was fascinating. Despite the recent proliferation of the wind turbines, the province of Ontario generated only a minimal quantity of electricity using wind energy. Almost half of the province's electricity came from nuclear power while twenty five percent or so was generated by hydroelectric plants.

As they continued on highway 401, Rakesh said, "I am going to ask you a weird question. Hope you won't mind."

"You've already asked me to move in with you. What could be any weirder?" Lina rebutted.

Rakesh rolled his eyes and was about to protest at her seemingly out of context claim, but Lina interrupted. "So, what's the weird question?"

"Well…," he hesitated, "It's about your differently colored eyes. How'd you get them?"

"Oh." Lina paused before continuing. "I got them from my father." She sounded sarcastic which perplexed Rakesh.

"So, you mean to say it was hereditary?" Rakesh asked.

"No, it was abuse."

"Excuse me?"

"My father had one of his ever so often rages and he hit me. Unfortunately, his blow landed on my left eye."

"Oh my gosh! When did this happen?" Rakesh asked incredulously.

"During the spring break little more than eight years ago; I was a senior in college."

"You were just a senior then? How old are you?"

"I am twenty-nine."

"Wow." Rakesh said, as he learned of her age for the first time. More importantly, he was trying to recall where he was when he was twenty-nine. It seemed like a long time ago.

"Wait a minute." Rakesh remembered something Lina had told him. "Didn't you say you don't have any family?"

"Yes, I did. I don't have a family. Not after that spring break. We all disowned each other and moved on with life. Well, at least, that's what I did."

"What happened?"

"It's a long story."

~~~   21   ~~~

"Have you heard of Toloby Homes?" Lina asked as they passed a decorative sign on the edge of highway 401. The sign indicated they were in the vicinity of Chatham-Kent, a mostly rural municipality encompassing populations of several towns, including Chatham, Tilbury, Ridgetown and Wallaceburg.

"Of course I have," replied Rakesh. "They are one of the largest home builders in the country, aren't they?"

"Yes, they are."

"I remember, when I looked for a house, the realtor took me around several homes built by Toloby. They were beautiful homes, but too much for my needs, and I ended up buying the condo. Mowing grass and shoveling snow aren't my cup of tea. Anyway, isn't it a privately owned company?"

"Yep. The owner's name is William Toloby."

"So, what's he got to do with you?" Rakesh asked with curiosity, wondering why she brought up Toloby Homes in the first place.

"I am his daughter." Lina replied.

Rakesh's eyes widened with abundant surprise. He turned toward her with disbelief. "You are what?"

"William Toloby is my father." Lina reiterated.

"That's interesting." Rakesh became immensely curious and he looked forward to hear the entire story.

Lina continued, "My father's father - my grandfather - Eugene Toloby founded Toloby Homes. He groomed my father to assume the reins of Toloby, and my father did just that as soon as my grandfather decided to pass on his legacy. My father had a ruthless passion for his company and grew the business by running a tight ship. Needless to say, he became worth millions in a short time, not to mention the guaranteed inheritance of millions more. He made my grandfather quite proud. Anyway, my father never strayed far away from the workings of every level of the organization. He made all the important decisions and expected everyone to fall in line to his whims. Unfortunately, he carried the same expectations in his personal life as well. As a man who was wealthy both by inheritance and self-made money, his circle of friends and acquaintances were all either truly wealthy or flaunted materialistic wealth. He met my mother somewhere in the middle of the money frenzy, claimed to have fallen in love, and married her. If I am to believe my mother, the real story happened to be that my mother was pretty much required to marry him to protect the inner circle of the wealthy."

"Anyway, soon they had me. How my father found time to get off of chasing money and procreate is beyond me, but here I was, their darling daughter who could be shown off to the society of the rich. As always, right from the beginning, decisions were made for me, most times by my father, or by my mother who happened to be directed by my father. In any case, he held the family leash - a damn short one."

"We lived in an expensive house, attended expensive parties, threw expensive parties, took expensive vacations and indulged in everything that looked and felt expensive. My parents never spared any expenses on me or on themselves. Why should they? With the housing market booming, anyone who walked into a bank could walk out with a mortgage. My father's company and everyone else in the construction business milked the fortune out of these good times. I recall my father proudly announcing his company's expansion into the Puerto Rican and Alaskan markets. I am not sure how many people needed new homes in Alaska, but he did it anyway. He called the whole thing the 'expansion into the extremes', whatever that meant. Toloby built homes in all types of land – foothills, mountains, deserts and swamps. In short, Toloby showed up wherever the zoning laws allowed."

"Yet, in the midst of multiplying wealth, I don't recall a single time my father bestowed true love to me. I was the only child; however, I don't recall a single hug, kiss or a close time together. When I watch you holding Madeline and playing silly games with her, I get jealous. If a person such as yourself could express love toward a child who is unrelated to you, why couldn't my dad to his own daughter? Anyway, my mother compensated my dad's deficiency with an affection which felt more like a pity than anything else. In the meantime, my dad traveled, worked hard, and brought work from home."

"Anytime he received word – and he did quite frequently - that I had disobeyed him or crossed some fictitious line he had drawn in his mind, he exploded in a maddening rage without any regard for my age or understanding of what I could or could not comprehend out of his rage. In the end, when I was really young, I shuddered in fear when my father had his moment of rage and my mother did her best to shield me. As I grew up and began understanding a lot more, I avoided my father as much as I could in an attempt to avoid his rage."

"Still, he managed to find a lot of things he disapproved of, and he somehow found me to vent his anger. In the beginning, his irrational anger happened to be in the form of yelling, but over time, became worse. He started hitting me anytime he got mad. Nothing aggressive to cause any serious physical injuries; nevertheless, his treatment of me only strengthened my resolve to continue to keep away from him. One time, I wrote a check with a typo. Instead of letting it go, I got yelled and beaten. Can you believe? Anyway, despite all these, my father never failed to shower me with anything and everything materialistic. Maybe he believed that the materialistic gifts compensated for his disgusting lack of parental skills."

"Where did you live at that time?" Rakesh asked, absorbing everything Lina said.

"Colorado Springs. Everyone called the place 'the Springs'. It's a beautiful city."

"South of Denver, correct?"

"Yep. It's located in the foothills of Pikes Peak, well, on the eastern edge of what's called the southern Rocky Mountains."

"Did you go to college there?"

"Yeah. I went to the University of Colorado in the Springs. I did my Bachelor's in Visual and Performing arts. And on the side, I learned commercial graphics, computerized design, web design and a few other things on my own. That's how I am where I am in my job as a graphics designer."

"I see. So, you left your family because of your father?"

"Well, there's more. First of all, I did not want to go to school at the University of Colorado, not because anything was wrong with the University, rather I wanted to get away as far as possible from my father. But my father enforced his rule. He said I must, if he were to pay for the four years of college. Having lived until then without the worries of money, I simply succumbed - once again. By this time, my fear of my father had escalated too. I imagined him inflicting all sorts of harm on me or my mother. So, one day, after I started my freshman year, I bought myself a digital voice recorder and kept it hidden at all times in my purse or somewhere on me. Somehow I thought it might be wise to record my father's rage which seemed to occur all too often. When I bought the gadget, I wasn't quite sure what I intended to do with it, but

I felt secure. Every time my father happened to be near me - yelling or otherwise, I turned the recorder and kept it on. Finally, in my senior year, the recorder proved its worth."

"It was also in my senior year that I met Brian. It was a cliché of a relationship. Rich girl and the poor boy, you know what I mean? Anyway, Brian worked for a contractor on a renovation project at the University. I think I've told you, he worked as an electrician. The construction site happened to be the adjacent building to my department. There was also an open area, like a courtyard, which looked more like a park, and the students hung around during breaks. I was one of them who frequented the courtyard. So did the construction workers. I bet the construction guys had a wonderful time relishing the eye candy - the young college girls. Then there was Brian. I noticed that he mostly kept to himself during his break. Of course, I only had a few occasions to pay attention to such things. In any event, one day I arbitrarily walked up to him and said hello, more to get some giggles out of the experience than anything serious. He looked up quite startled, looked around and then smiled. He said hello back to me. We introduced ourselves, started chatting about nothing in particular. That was the beginning."

"Over time, we formally began dating; well, at least that's what I am claiming we did. In all practical terms, we had a difficult time finding time to be alone and together. For one, Brian worked long hours and went home tired. On the other hand, I had a ton of schoolwork, projects, and my father's 'to do' regimen, if I were to keep him less rabid. But Brian and I did manage to find time every now and then and got to know each other more. As our relationship grew, so did my fears. I knew, no way in hell my father would approve of Brian. So, I hid our growing relationship from him. But, I shared those fears with Brian, and at the time, I don't think for one moment, he grasped the enormity of my situation. He simply said time would solve all the conundrums. Yes, for him, time solved everything."

"The following year, when the spring semester of my senior year began, Brian mentioned that his assignment at the renovation project was over and he was going back to resume his full time employment with his company. I didn't quite understand what he meant; he always had strange employment arrangements anyway. From that point on, I had a more difficult time trying to meet him as our schedules conflicted. Yet, we maintained a close relationship. He became officially my boyfriend and the first one with whom I had a serious relationship. When his assignment at the University ended, Brian suggested we meet at a location next to the home construction site where he worked. The site was a new sub-division monopolized by two major home builders. One of them turned out to be Toloby Homes."

"Wow. Let me guess. Was Brian working for Toloby Homes?" Rakesh asked as he took the ramp to the rest stop on highway 401. The rest stops, recently upgraded with new facilities, were named 'onroute'.

"Yes, indeed. Can you believe?"

Rakesh parked his vehicle. He took Madeline out of her child seat; she seemed to have had enough of being cramped in the seat. They all walked into the building, purchased something light to eat, and settled in for a few minutes of break. Madeline ran around free for a while.

Moments later, they resumed their drive toward Toronto.

"So, let me get this. You had a boyfriend. He worked for your father's company. You pretty much figured out that your father would oppose this relationship and therefore you didn't tell him. How did this all work out?" Rakesh asked after summarizing what Lina told him so far.

"It worked out into my differently colored eyes which I have now." Lina replied with a sarcastic grin.

"Got it. Now, I am truly intrigued to know the rest of the story."

"Well, when Brian told me he worked for Toloby Homes, I told him who I was to Toloby. He began to understand why I had told him that my father would never approve of the relationship. Anyway, the chips started falling in its place soon after. One day during my spring break, I went to the site and waited for Brian to wrap up his day's work. One of the Toloby Homes' Supervisors, present at the site as part of his routine, recognized me. As a matter of courtesy to his boss's daughter, he asked if I needed any assistance. I didn't know him and I told him I was there to meet Brian. He acknowledged and walked away. However, I believe a few minutes later, he may have seen me and Brian together. He might have put two and two together and concluded a story of his own in his head. That was my best guess anyway. Regardless, my father learned about us two and he confronted me."

"He burst into my room and went into an instant rage. He asked me who the guy was and what he had to do with me. The voice recorder was on. I gave him all the details, at least everything until he managed to stand still and listen to me, which was not for too long. He yelled, screamed, huffed, puffed, and paced back and forth in my room saying all sorts of things a decent human being wouldn't utter. Finally, he gave me the cinematic ultimatum – I should stop seeing him and put an end to this nonsense. I categorically refused. He asked me what I intended to do. I told him I would continue to date him and if everything worked out, marry him. Of course, Brian might have flipped out on those last few words of mine as we, at that time, never ventured our discussion to any mention of marriage. In any event, upon hearing the word marriage, my father went berserk and completely out of control.

"My father told me, at the highest decibel level he could muster without giving himself a heart attack, that he would never allow the marriage and in fact he would put an end to our relationship right away. I told him to go suck rock since I didn't care anymore about what he thought or said. Of course, he got madder. He walked toward me, raised his hand with a full fist and aimed, I believe at my shoulders. I am not sure. I ducked instinctively and his punch landed right on my left eye. I fell on the floor and heard my mother for the first time during this fiasco. She stood there screaming in pure terror. I, in the meantime, found the energy to stand back up. My father meanwhile, fully prepared, launched another punch toward me. This time, I was prepared. I fended off his punch, grabbed his arm, and bit him. Yeah, I bit him so hard that the bastard howled like a dog stuck in a trap."

"You bit him?" Rakesh asked incredulously.

"Yes, I did. My father backed off and I could see blood on his arm."

"Anyway, in a few minutes, cops were all over my parents' house. My mother must have called 911. The cops noticed my bruised left eye and my father's bloodied arm, asked what happened, and wondered whom to place under arrest for assault. Ambulances, fire trucks, and the whole nine yards arrived to take care of us multi-millionaires who couldn't behave like normal human beings."

"My father meanwhile made an instant transformation into a respectable elitist and tried to convince the cops that everything was hunky dory in the household. Of course, the cops weren't stupid. They probably saw this kind of thing every day inside those mansions. So, they refused to leave until they could dig up the whole story. However, after an intense private discussion between my father and the cops, everyone decided not to charge anyone, and the household was indeed hunky dory after all. No police reports were written – something I learned later on – and no one was arrested. Everyone supposedly agreed that things would be better off if left quiet. After all, who wants a scandal? The only official evidence of any abnormality was the 911 call from my mother."

"In the meantime, my voice recorder recorded the entire chaos without anyone knowing about it besides me. After the cops left, my father, much calmer by now, only because of exhaustion than anything else, issued this menacing threat – if I continued my relationship with Brian even for one more second, he would fire Brian from Toloby Homes. I told him I fully intended to ignore his bullshit threat. I also told him of my impromptu decision to leave him, my mother, and the rest of the family with no plans on ever returning. My voice recorder recorded this as well."

"Over the next few days, my left eye continued to bother me along with the pain on my cheekbone. The doctor told me I had suffered a blunt blow to the eye; not a revelation at all after having experienced the stuff first hand. The doctor did not however know the possible after effects. A short time later, the doctor detected hemorrhaging in my left eye which he concluded was due to the blunt blow. Other than periodic pangs of pain which could not be clearly diagnosed, nothing seemed out of the ordinary. My vision stayed as normal as possible and I did not experience any side effects or consequences of the blow from that day. What I did notice after almost six months was a subtle difference in the color of my left eye. I again visited my doctor who did not find anything abnormal in my eye although he detected the slight variation in the color of my iris. That's when he said I might end up with a condition called hetero something."

"Heterochromia," offered Rakesh.

"Yep, that's the one. Over several more months, my iris changed to a distinct hazel, the one I have now."

"Well, gosh, I am appalled at the things which happened to you because of your father. That must not have been easy for you," said Rakesh.

"Well, I am over it now. Seems like a long time ago."

"You know, if it's any consolation, your eyes, the ones you have now, are beautiful. They're exotic," said Rakesh.

Lina turned her head, looked at Rakesh, and rolled her eyes. Then she realized that he meant what he said and muttered, "Well, thanks."

"So, did you leave home and everyone as you said you would?" Rakesh asked.

"Of course I did. I wasn't sure what I had in mind; I just walked toward the front door to walk away with whatever I had on me at the time. My mother, still very much sobbing, stopped me and pleaded for me to change my mind. I refused. Finally, she gave in and told me I could leave, but she wanted to pack me few essentials and some money. She asked me where I planned to go and I told her - to Brian's house. Thankfully, I knew where he lived. I also told my mother not to contact me anymore. Now, looking back, I think that was too harsh on my mother, but at that time, my mother meekly agreed. Maybe she came to grips that I would be better off without them. She packed two suitcases of clothes, handed me two thousand dollars cash and called a cab. So, yeah, I didn't leave with just what I had on me, but with something to survive. Since then, I have never gone back or have contacted my parents, family, or anyone else for that matter. Neither have they."

"When Brian saw me at his apartment doorstep with two suitcases plus a bruised and bandaged left eye, he must have guessed what happened. He didn't say a word. He grabbed my suitcases, put them in a corner, escorted me inside his house, and gave me the most comforting hug I've ever experienced. Finally, I lost my composure. I broke down in a river of tears and must have wept for the next couple of hours. Brian had his arms around me and said nothing. Coming to think of, he must have been terrified. After we were married, I used to ask him what he thought of that day; he refused to discuss. Anyway, that night, I slept on his bed and he slept on the couch."

"The next day, Brian left for work early as he always did and I woke up to what would be the reality of my life from that day forward. My father in the meantime likely learned from my mother that I left them for Brian. I wasn't there to witness firsthand his torrent of rage, which I am sure occurred and directed to the next scapegoat – my mother. I however witnessed the consequences of his outrage. Brian returned from work around nine in the morning which, needless to say, was outright unusual for a man who didn't show up home until almost after six or seven in the evening. Toloby Homes had terminated his employment. They gave him no reason other than the fact that his services were no longer required. Another hundred or so new homes needed electrical work, but hey, Brian's services were not required. My father kept his promise of firing Brian."

"I told Brian everything that happened the previous day including my father's threat. I didn't tell him about the voice recorder. Brian absorbed them quietly. A bit later, he told me he would contact some contractor he knew and try to find work. He also said everything would be alright over time; another one of his 'time is the solution' speech."

"In the meantime, I had no intention of sitting around and let my father screw Brian's career. So, I paced back and forth, and came up with a sinister list of things to do. First, I made a phone call to the 'Problem Solvers' team at the Springs' local news. I told them Toloby Homes had just violated the State's employment laws by wrongfully terminating an employee. They became interested to hear more and I provided them all the details including the recording of my father's threat to fire Brian. They loved every bit, considering the whole thing came straight from the mouth of the owner's daughter. Who wouldn't? They dispatched one of the guys off the team, along with cameras and such, to interview me. I happily sang for the cameras and played the voice recorder which was filled with my father's hateful madness. Besides, my bruised and bandaged eye charmed the camera."

"To add some spice, I told them how my father punched me and in defense, how I bit him. I told them about the cops and what they did and didn't do. A second later, I had this light bulb moment. I told the 'Problem Solvers' that the cops didn't take any action at the behest of my father. In other words, I alleged a cover up by the police whom, I said, took the side of my father, the rich man in the town. Of course, I couldn't prove a cover up, but everything else happened to be true. Delighted with the juicy details, the 'Problem Solvers' profusely thanked me for the story and promised to air everything at prime time."

"Soon after the TV crew left, I contacted the office of the State Attorney General. After punching through the myriad of options, I finally spoke to a staff member and reported a police cover up of an assault at the residence of William Toloby. I didn't stop there. I dug up the names and phone numbers of the city council members and managed to actually speak to two of them. I told them the same thing – a cover up by the police. Interestingly enough, as soon as I mentioned the name Toloby, I received one hundred percent attention."

"Oh, my god! You were spiteful," exclaimed Rakesh.

"Yes, of course. I decided not to let Brian suffer because of our dysfunctional family situation. There's more. I got in touch with the Colorado Department of Labor and reported the wrongful dismissal of Brian and gave them too the whole story. Once done with all of these, I sat around and waited to find out how lethal the explosion would turn out to be."

"Was Brian home when the press came to interview you?"

"No, he had stepped out to meet the contractor that he mentioned about, and he didn't get home until around four or five, I think. After he came home, I told him about the press, the voice recorder, and my allegation of police cover up. To my surprise, he started laughing hysterically as he couldn't believe what I said. He thought I was blurting out some nonsense. Then he listened to the entire recording on the voice recorder and he sat there and shook his head in disbelief."

"In the evening, we both grabbed a beer and turned on the six o'clock local news to find out what would be reported. The 'Problem Solvers' decided to skip the problem solving segment altogether.

Instead, they made it the breaking news of the evening. It was fantastic to hear my father's recording of his yells and threats as they televised on the news channel. After my interview in the morning, the news outlet had contacted Toloby Homes and apparently had told them of the planned airing. Needless to say, Toloby scrambled a mouthpiece whose job was to bullshit some nonsense in the name of defending the company. So, there he was, Jack Waltenberger was his name, making a jackass of himself on the camera trying to dodge the reporter's questions. He clearly couldn't deny the recording as he knew Toloby Homes was caught with its pants down."

"The other interesting part was my allegation of police cover up. The reporter, of course, had contacted the police department for a comment and as a result, the spokesperson showed up on the camera as he tried to figure out what the hell happened between the officers and my father. On top of all, my bandaged eye did not do anything to put the police or the jackass Jack in a favorable light."

"For the next couple of days, the frenzy was alive and well. The news of a scandal at Toloby Homes had spread all the way to Denver where Toloby had a significant presence. The Springs Mayor's office and the State Attorney General's office issued their own 'on the record' comments on this issue, but didn't seem to be too involved. However, by the end of the week, the Labor Department announced an investigation of the employment practices at Toloby Homes."

"In the meantime, the local news did a live interview of Brian and he was just as delighted to talk to the media. My father, for his part stayed off the limelight and didn't say a word. He probably hoped that this would just die a natural death which after almost two weeks did not. I think the only reason it did not was because the police were determined to investigate my allegation of cover up. They probably thought that they were unfairly caught up in this mess. They now investigated my father. This I think finally flushed him out of his mansion cave. He came on camera with a prepared speech which was nothing but eloquent. He regretted the entire incident but denied any wrongdoing. I am not sure what he meant by the incident – the altercation with me, the hush-hush discussion with the police, or the firing of Brian. His attorney and other important minions stood at his side and shook their heads in unified agreement as my father spoke."

"My father's press statement roused Brian from his normally stoic demeanor. He left his apartment; said something about talking to an attorney. Anyway, the next day Brian told me he was suing Toloby Homes for wrongful dismissal. We made sure the media knew about the lawsuit, and that revived the frenzy for a few more days. Brian's attorney, a flamboyant piece of work, was just that - he was flamboyant and nothing else. He summoned an elaborate press conference and derided Toloby Homes to such an extent he could have gotten sued for defamation. But his theatrics did the trick. Toloby made another pitiful attempt to put this all behind; as a result, they once again made a public appearance. Jackass Jack returned to TV declaring that Brian would get his employment back if all parties calmed down and settled this matter outside of the courts. Brian told Toloby to shove their offer up their rear end; the lawsuit would not be dropped."

"It took another couple of months for the attorneys from the two sides to rib each other and finally negotiate an out of court monetary settlement. I have no idea what happened to the police investigation of the cover up or the Labor Department's investigation. Once Brian got compensated by the settlement, we both lost interest, and Brian suggested that we move out of Colorado Springs. Of course, I had to finish my degree program and I still had a month or so. So, we held on to the Springs until then. I attended classes while living with Brian. He wasn't used to the constant presence of a woman and was funny to watch him cope with me. Meanwhile, his lawsuit settlement was a significant chunk and he was happy. He also found a contract job and did okay on money."

"The days passed mostly uneventful and my semester finally came to an end. Then my father came back in our lives to haunt us again. By then, he knew where I lived. One day, I received a certified mail from his attorney demanding I pay back all the tuition and fee my father paid for me to attend the University. He threatened a lawsuit if I didn't pay back. I was shocked, but not surprised. Clearly, I didn't have any money of my own; so I talked to Brian. He simply wrote me a check out of the money he received from the lawsuit settlement and I mailed it to my father. In a convoluted way, we paid back my father using his own money. After this, we truly hoped we wouldn't have to deal with my father or any of my family anymore."

"What about Brian's family? Where were they?" Rakesh asked.

"I have no clue. Brian claimed he left home at a young age and he refused to talk about it. He never discussed and quite honestly, I didn't care. He was there for me and nothing else mattered to me."

Lina continued, "I graduated in summer and we left town. Brian came to know of a major commercial construction slated to begin that summer. This was in Lincoln, Nebraska. He contacted somebody who put him in touch with someone else and in the end found himself a job to do all the electrical work. The work was guaranteed for at least fifteen months. So, we packed up, rented a U-Haul, and moved to Lincoln. While Brian left for work, I searched for work. Fresh out of college, I ended up in the 'chicken or egg' situation. Employers looked for experience and so was I. Finally, I landed an entry level position, bought my own car, and felt a sense of belonging. That's also when Brian proposed to me. We got married shortly after in a family court with neither of our families attending. A couple of years later, we had Makenzie."

Lina paused. Then she said, "Makie was also very close to Brian. She was his baby."

Rakesh nodded realizing that Lina was recalling the painful memories of the school shooting. After a moment of silence, Lina asked, "Do you know how Makie's name was spelled?"

"M-a-c-k-e-n-z-i-e." Rakesh spelled, wondering what now.

"Supposedly, that's the normal spelling. Anyway, we screwed it up while filling out the form at the hospital after she was born. Our Makie did not have a C after M and A. We didn't realize until we went to the city office to obtain the birth certificate."

"Did you live in Lincoln for a long time?"

"No, Brian's assignment got over in about eighteen months and we moved. I quit my job and we went to Kansas City in Missouri. For some bizarre reason, we figured we needed to move at least a couple of hundred miles from the previous location. We had the urge to eliminate all possible traces of us from the previous places we lived. Anyway, it just felt good to move far away."

"Here in Kansas City, we bought our first home. We put the lawsuit settlement money, or whatever remained of it, as down payment. We enjoyed living in our own home, but didn't live in it for too long. We seemed to relish a semi-nomadic lifestyle. Thereafter, we lived in St. Louis and Nashville before working our way up to Columbus and then finally here to Beniton Heights. We sold and bought new homes in Nashville and Columbus, and we lived in a rental condo in St. Louis. And here I am, ready to sell my house all over again. During all this selling and buying of houses, we lost money on some and evened out on others, but never made any money. I became indifferent to money a long time ago, as I felt, well, I still feel, that money never brought me happiness. I had lived amid obscene wealth, yet had to suffer my father's abuse. That alone was enough to make money a turn-off for me. Meanwhile, Brian wasn't too careful with money; we made enough to survive and even live a fairly comfortable life, but ended up going into debt here and there, which you now know all about. Anyway, this is my story from Colorado Springs to Beniton Heights."

They reached Woodstock where they decided to stop at another service area. Rakesh's plan was to drive to Oakville, check into the hotel, drop their bags, and take the GO train to the Union Station in downtown Toronto. After a twenty five minute break at the Woodstock service area, they resumed their drive. Within a few kilometers, the fork for highway 403 appeared. Rakesh switched to the right most lanes to get to 403 which would take them to Oakville, before reaching Toronto. They would pass the cities of Brantford, Hamilton, and Burlington before arriving in Oakville.

After riding in silence for an extended time period, Lina suddenly said, "Hey, we should eat something authentically Canadian!"

"What? Did you suddenly have an epiphany?" Rakesh teased her.

"No, I am serious. Is there something which is considered Canadian?"

"Hmm. Let me think. Well, here is one. Do you know what poutine is?"

"The who?"

"Not who. It's a what. Poutine is a dish which originated in Quebec and can be found all across Canada. Anyway, it is French fries covered with cheese curds and topped with brown gravy."

"It does not sound appetizing at all. Have you had it anytime?" Lina asked.

"No, I haven't. I heard about poutine from one of my Canadian co-worker. He said he's had it at local fast food joints."

"Won't the fries become soggy and yucky with all the curd and gravy?"

"I think they put the curd and gravy when they are ready to serve the food. But hey, what do I know? I am not the scholar of culinary sciences. I thrive on frozen food."

"So, do you think we can find poutine in Toronto?"

"Of course. Should we try?" Rakesh asked.

"I am all for it," agreed Lina.

~~~   22   ~~~

The initial months of the New Year marked the completion of a number of planned tasks which kept both Lina and Rakesh busy all along. True to its reputation, Beniton Heights continued to remain a destination of choice for those seeking a new home, and as an evidence of the popularity, by the end of February, Lina's home was bought out by another young family. The sale provided an immense relief for Lina, not only because of the freedom from an unaffordable mortgage, but it also helped infuse her almost negligible savings with some emergency cash.

In the days before her home's sale, Lina had several items related to her financial situation that had to be put to bed and Rakesh lent a hand on each of those items. This allowed him a number of opportunities to visit her and Madeline at their home. In mid-January, during one such visit to her home, they reviewed a fresh set of monthly bills. One of them happened to be the credit card bill with the charge from the crematorium. By January, additional finance charges had accumulated on top of few other transactions, resulting in an outstanding balance of little over five thousand dollars. After they were finished with the other bills, as he was about to leave, without uttering a word, Rakesh grabbed the credit card statement and stowed it in his pocket.

Rakesh made the decision to pay off her credit card and inform Lina later. He was in no mood to face her objections. Rakesh also sat down with her, and together, created a budget. The mortgage remained a burden; however, both Lina and Rakesh remained confident of a quick sale as there was considerable interest from prospective buyers. Their confidence proved right when the house was sold a month later.

In the meantime, it didn't take long for Lina to figure out that something was amiss with the credit card bill. When she received her February statement, she found a lump sum payment posted on the account. She did not recall ever making a payment for such an amount;

she did not have the money in the first place to make the payment. Suspecting the obvious, she confronted Rakesh who in turn admitted his action. Lina became furious. She was furious over what she considered as Rakesh's attempt to undermine her financial independence, and at her own inability to afford the current lifestyle. Venting her fury, she vowed to pay him back – not just the amount from the credit card, but also the mortgage payments which Rakesh made on her behalf. Not wishing to aggravate the situation, Rakesh agreed to accept the repayment if she so wished. Lina rebutted by stating it was not a matter of 'if', but 'when'.

Rakesh held up his hands in surrender.

The initial months also brought in a fresh and quite exhilarating perspective into Rakesh's life. He was astonished at the extent of attachment Madeline displayed toward him. He did not comprehend whether Madeline substituted him for her father or simply bonded to a new person with whom her mother spent quite a bit of time. Either way, Rakesh always looked forward to spend time with the little girl. Lina appreciated the care Rakesh provided to Madeline. She watched with amusement the games that Rakesh conjured for her daughter. Every time Rakesh engaged the child, it allowed Lina to relax and rest a bit. Despite that, Lina could not yet let herself trust Rakesh completely. Therefore, she remained conflicted and never let Madeline with Rakesh without her presence. On occasion, when Rakesh offered to pick Madeline from the daycare, Lina politely declined. Rakesh's home, in the meantime, went through an evolution from a bachelor pad to a child friendly abode.

Lina's home had a new and confirmed buyer during the first week of February and the closing was set for the end of February. This also meant that time was running out for Lina to make a decision regarding her future home. After a prolonged contemplation, she decided to choose Rakesh's third option; Lina and Madeline would live in Rakesh's condominium. The prominent factor that influenced her decision was Madeline's seemingly tight knit bond with Rakesh which only seemed to grow stronger as the days passed. Despite her less than perfect trust of Rakesh, Lina felt it might not hurt to allow Madeline enjoy a father figure in her life. After all, if things failed to work out after moving in, Lina had the choice to exercise other options without any encumbrance.

Lina conveyed her decision to Rakesh; he was elated. To begin with however, she wanted to set a few conditions. First, she would pay rent for living in his home. Almost immediately, Rakesh and Lina embarked on a frivolous argument for a few minutes as to what the rent amount would be. Her next condition – she be allowed to contribute to the household expenses. Rakesh agreed under the condition that she contribute only within her means. Lina also warned him not to meddle with, or pay her credit card bills. Rakesh agreed with a grin. Since not all of Lina's household items could fit in Rakesh's condo, they made arrangements to rent a storage unit until such time when further decisions on habitation could be made.

In March, Lina and Madeline arrived at Rakesh's home and settled in as cohabiting tenants.

Within a few days, Rakesh realized it was far easier to offer his home and heart to two others than to adjust to the new personalities that the two brought with them. Such things were not quite evident during the entire time Lina and Madeline spent with Rakesh since, at the end of the day, they left him and his home for himself. However, now, his home became theirs as well. This brought a stark realization that it was going to take a while for him to acclimatize to the new arrangement. The first of the many luxuries of bachelorhood to vanish from Rakesh's life was his extended sleeping hours during weekends, something entirely caused by Madeline. He discovered no matter how exhausted Madeline was, or how deep of a slumber she was in, the little girl was always up and hyperactive by seven in the morning. Unfortunately for Rakesh, Madeline channeled her lively spirits toward Rakesh by walking into his bedroom first thing in the morning with an expectation to be entertained.

Lina on the other hand found his home too bare. She began populating the walls and the corners with hangings and other decorative items she previously had in her home. She made a conscious effort to avoid bringing in too many items for fears of triggering memories of the past. Rakesh, for the most part, remained neutral on Lina's penchant for the wall hangings and other displays, but deep inside, he knew his choices would have been vastly different from hers if he had a say in the matter.

Lina found Rakesh's inventory of Indian culinary raw materials to be too confusing, overly aromatic, and excessively spicy for her tastes. She found herself sniffing almost everything in an attempt to pinpoint their identities, and in the process ended up in bouts of sneezing and coughing. Within a short period of time, Rakesh's pantry and the refrigerator went through a dramatic transformation by means of fresh food, groceries, and other items which represented the diversity of the condo's inhabitants. Although Lina gave her best efforts to try Indian food, and enjoyed a majority of them, she drew a line at the level of spiciness. As a result, the Indian dishes fell several notches below in flavor than what Rakesh normally preferred.

The condo's ground level – the so called basement – turned into a toy haven, and Madeline splurged amid them. There were also additional furniture and other household items which belonged to Lina; most of them failed to match with the existing paltry décor. After a few attempts of mixing and matching the items with the décor, both Lina and Rakesh gave up and let the items be the way they were. The condo's garage was big enough to fit only one vehicle and so did the driveway. Therefore, both the adults needed to remember not to double-park and block each other. Since Rakesh normally left for work earlier than Lina did, he ended up parking his car in one of the common parking spaces on the street. This resulted in Rakesh spending additional time defrosting or scraping the windows and the windshield on cold mornings; something he hadn't had to do all these years. He griped and dealt with it in silence.

The trivial task of watching TV went through a transformation of its own. Lina assumed the role of the minder and scrutinized the programs which Rakesh habitually enjoyed. She wanted to ensure the appropriateness of the programs' contents when Madeline was present. As the not so subtle censorship became the norm, Rakesh found himself watching more of kids' channels than anything else. Lina graciously exempted few programs on Discovery and History channels. Over time, Rakesh adjusted to the updated viewing list by consoling himself that he was better off learning the cartoon characters than be glued to some cartoonish media which spewed nothing more than sensationalism under the pretext of journalism.

Another unexpected fact was the extent to which his household machineries operated. The washer and the dryer had never experienced a running time such as now, for, Madeline seemed to consume clothes beyond Rakesh's imagination. For instance, she went to the daycare spotless and returned home grimy. The same applied to the kitchenware. The consumption of cutlery and other kitchen utensils seemed to be relentless, resulting in an overtime run mode of the dishwasher.

Madeline seemed to be the most content of the three. She couldn't be any happier. She had her mom and she had Rakesh; she wasn't quite clear of her relationship to him, but adored his company. In the end, despite several quirky inconveniences – both real and perceived, Lina and Rakesh took major efforts to accommodate each other and gave their best to maintain peace. After all, for the most part, they both enjoyed the company of the other, and therefore, did not find the need to pursue any trivial arguments.

~~~   23   ~~~

One month of cohabitation passed by successfully. The two maintained their routines and stayed clear of anything which could lead to petty arguments. The clocks sprung ahead an hour in Beniton Heights. The days became noticeably longer while the nights remained cold. On one such late evening, as in many others, Madeline was off to bed, and Rakesh was on his couch watching TV. This was his time with the least level of censorship. He flipped through the channels to land on something suitable for his taste. Lina made herself some hot chocolate and offered some to Rakesh who declined. She was wearing a brushed cotton poplin pajama button-up shirt and pants. The pajama was covered with tropical blooms, palm trees, and Tikis. Lina walked over to the living room with her cup of hot chocolate and sat on the couch next to Rakesh. She settled down close enough to him that her knees touched him as she put her legs up on the couch. He could smell the pleasant aroma of the skin lotion she had on her.

Then the awkwardness settled upon Rakesh. He was too close to her, or vice versa. Lina, however, seemed to be neither unperturbed nor discomforted at the apparent deprivation of Rakesh's personal space. Regardless, he instinctively moved a bit away from her, and Lina instantly noticed. She took her eyes off the TV and turned her head to look at him. At this close proximity, he found her heterochromatic eyes all the more beautiful.

"Don't worry," Lina said with a serious but sarcastic expression, "I am not going to molest you!"

Rakesh let out a chuckle and rolled his eyes.

"So, tell me, why are you still a bachelor?" Lina asked; her manner of pursuing a conversation often involved abrupt changes in topic.

"What?" Rakesh asked, a bit startled at the choice of her conversational topic.

"You heard me. How come you are a bachelor? You are good

looking with that manly mustache and all. Are you seeing anyone?"

Rakesh burst out laughing. "I am glad you are impressed with my mustache. Anyway, no, I am not seeing anyone, and I have no idea why I am still a bachelor. Do you think something is wrong with me?"

"How the hell am I supposed to know? But, I am going to tell you one thing. It's going to be hard for you to find a mate while living with a female roommate and her child. Don't you think?"

"Point well taken. But, I think I'll worry about the little technicality if and when I do have to bring a mate home with me. The way things are at the moment, that possibility is more of an 'if' than a 'when'."

"Why do you say so? Is it because of me and Madie?"

"No, hell no. Of course not."

"So, what do you mean by 'the way things are'?"

"Well, the whole thing is kind of complicated. First of all, I can't see myself being married. Seems to me like a lot of trouble. You know how it is - wife, obligations, nonsense, etc."

"Wow, you went from wife to nonsense in the same sentence. That doesn't help."

Rakesh laughed. "You know what I mean. Then my mom, bless her heart, doesn't know when to quit. She continues to send me pictures and details of prospective brides; girls who supposedly are willing to marry me. That completely turns me off. So I use immigration as an excuse to ward her off. Anyway, that's what I meant by 'the way things are right now'."

"Whoa. Wait, wait. Slow down. This is interesting. You got me all bamboozled. What pictures of brides are you talking about and what's with immigration?"

"You are familiar with the practice of arranged marriages in India? Aren't you?"

"Yeah, sort of."

"Alright, here's the super high level version of the marriage protocol. I might be wrong to a certain extent as quite a bit might have changed for better or worse, but this is the version I am familiar with. First of all, my parents – my mom more than my dad – were under the strong notion that I should be married by mid-twenties. Clearly, that did not happen, and they freaked out when I turned thirty as a bachelor. That's when the pictures of the eligible bachelorettes began showing up in my mailbox, and I am talking about the US Postal Service mailbox. These days, they are in my email."

"Anyway, on the conservative side of things, the initial steps begin with a bunch of information transfer about the boy and the girl. The parents of both sides test the interests of each other. Mind you, at this point, these two parties in most cases are complete strangers attached perhaps by the strings of religion, caste, sub-castes and what not. At some point, idle chatter and information sharing turns into serious inquiry. The boy's parents are interested, among other things, in a girl who is homely, God fearing, modest, a good cook, etc. In other words, they are seeking a girl with subservient characteristics who will do the bidding of her future husband and in-laws. Let's not forget the crazy preference for a girl with a light complexioned skin tone. You people are desperate to get tanned and we people are desperate to get light. The girl's parents on the other hand are keenly interested in the professional standing of the boy in preferred occupations. If the guy works and lives outside of India, it is another plus, never mind the false sense of superiority surrounding it. Anyway, the earnings of the boy are freely divulged, padded, and embellished. Fancier the job title, the better it is for both the boy and his proud parents. The current or the former professional standing of the boy's father also plays an important role. Status is almost everything. After all, what would the society say if a rich girl ends up marrying an electrician?"

Lina glared at Rakesh, and a moment later, let out a loud laugh. "Spoken like a true Toloby," she remarked.

Rakesh continued, "Anyway, by now, pictures and bio-data of several are exchanged. Bio-data is a résumé of sorts, only with a lot more personal information than you care to share. Once the list is narrowed down to a manageable few, the families exchange the horoscopes of the boy and the girl. The charts on the horoscope are developed based on the time, place, and date of birth. Professional astrologers are everywhere making a killing out of the matrimonial market. They seek certain traits which supposedly tell them whether or not the couple's union would be a happy and a permanent one. The list is then narrowed down further. By this time, an approved shortlist of boys and girls is generated – a list approved by everyone other than the boys and the girls themselves. Finally, the list is declassified and sent to the wards. In my case, this is the list in my possession – a list which has been through professional and critical vetting; guaranteed to satisfy me. Of course, my parents are not at all extremely conservative; but, in the absence of my cooperation, they have resorted to what they feel is the best."

"Over the years, the protocol has evolved as well, and the entire affair may have become less conservative in a number of circumstances. For one, the internet is loaded with matrimonial websites. Profiles of the boy and the girl are posted with and without the boy or the girl's consent. With the advent of the web, the parents are able to cast the net farther in search of the perfect mate. Also, the unmarried themselves post their profile, thereby earning the gratification of selecting their own mate. The selection is usually submitted for parental approval. The other effect of the evolution is the fact that the requirements of sub-caste, caste, religion, region, language, etc., are often overlooked. Parents are willing, or in increasingly many cases, forced to consider partners for their sons and daughters from a community that is different from them. The parents make up for this sacrilege by either declaring themselves as modern or blame everything on the wretched influence of the foreign culture."

"Then, there's the so called progressive group of unmarried who simply go ahead, choose their partner, and inform of their decision to the family. Mind you, they are not asking for permission; they are well beyond that stage by then. I am not sure how much of this is occurring in India, but I am aware of a number of them who live here and have pursued this path. In a number of cases, the parents go through the stages of denial to an all-out offensive before resigning to the inevitable."

"I remember a friend of mine – this was around six years ago – who decided to get married to an Indian girl – a coworker of his. His parents on the other hand vehemently objected. In a bizarre sequence of events, his parents secretly lined up a girl of their preference just before he was flying to India for a random visit. Their intent was to corner him and force him to marry the girl they had picked. Well, I heard later that the entire episode went down in a dramatic fiasco when he landed in India and learned about it a day later. Among many things, he told the girl's parents – since they were complicit in this sneaky arrangement - he would contact the US embassy and press charges of immigration fraud against the girl. I am not sure how much they believed in his bullshit threat, but they backed off not wanting to risk their daughter's future."

"Now, I must say, amid this bright cocktail of practices, there are parents who truly don't believe in any of what I said till now, and agree to their son or daughter's choice of the partner without much of a fuss or fanfare. But, I think that is still a minority. In my case, my mom has not given up. Every time I speak to my parents, my mom brings up this topic and whines. In any event, she has evolved with the times as well. Courtesy of my mom, my profile is now on couple of matrimonial sites, and according to her, receives regular feedback from interested parties. She has relaxed her criteria as well; now, her search pans the entire nation of India. In the end, I continue to receive photos and such on a regular basis. So, that's the story of the bride emails and photos. I should perhaps show some of those to you and you can suggest a suitable one to be my wife. What do you say?"

"Uh-huh," replied Lina with a grin. "So, how is this all related to immigration?"

"Well, immigration is another convoluted thing I can talk about for days. Here's how the law works for a person such as myself who is a green card holder. If I marry a foreign citizen aka one of the photo brides, I can't bring my wife to the US right away, unless of course she happens to be here legally on her own status such as a student or a full time employee. I have to first apply to sponsor my wife and those applications are under a backlog which would take more than a good chunk of time before the sponsorship is approved.

"Why?" Lina asked incredulously.

"Well, that happens to be the law. When I sponsor a spouse, the application gets filed in a queue with annual numerical limits. Needless to say, there is more demand for green card than there is availability. The availability therefore is determined by what's called the priority date. This is the date the application is received and stamped by US immigration. One needs to wait until the priority date becomes current; in other words, an immigrant visa should become available for the applicant. Similar to employment-based green card applications, the numerical limits are set for each country. So, for someone born in India, the current wait time to obtain a green card, I think is few months. It used to be a couple of years. Of course, the wait time is unpredictable and can change anytime for better or worse. This elaborate and confusing explanation has so far discouraged my mom from pushing me beyond forcing me to look at the photos and the details."

"Goodness gracious. This is ridiculous. So, if I want to marry a handsome Russian, is this what I need to go through?" Lina asked teasingly.

"Depends on which catalog you are choosing the Russian from." Rakesh replied with a straight face.

"What?"

"I am just kidding. Your case would be a little different. You are a US citizen. If a US citizen marries a foreign citizen, the sponsorship does not come under the numerical limits or quota. So, the spouse can join the other within a short time."

"I see. Aren't you going to become a US citizen?"

"Yes, I do intend to become one, and I am almost eligible to do so."

"After you become one, you won't have this excuse, would you?"

"Not this one. But I am sure I can come up with another."

"Or, you could simply agree to your mom and get married," concluded Lina.

"Really? Just like that? Pick one from the photo lineup and get married? I don't think so," rebutted Rakesh.

"You know what? I think you are more scared of commitment than you are of the pictures of the brides. Am I right?"

"Kind of."

Lina sighed. "You don't like to talk about it too much, do you?"

"Not really," said Rakesh laughing. "Look, I don't know why I haven't gotten married. Maybe, it's indeed my fear of commitment or fear of additional responsibilities. I don't think too much about these things. I am sure, if I reflect deep enough, I'll find out the reason."

Lina said, "Do you realize, in the past few months, you have voluntarily changed your lifestyle from a bachelor to a pseudo-married man with a child? I mean, this is like some form of spontaneous combustion. One day, you are lazing around all by yourself in this house and the next day you end up with us in your life and before you know, we are actually living with you. Just think about it. Madeline adores you and she seems to spend more time with you than with me. She doesn't let you sleep-in and you put up. You are now also an expert at changing her diapers without throwing up at the smell of her poop. You change her clothes and feed her. Then of course, you got me constantly hovering in your presence. We all go out together – shop, watch movies, eat out, and more. You are already doing what most married people do. Well, at least most of it, if you know what I mean."

Rakesh said, "I guess you are right. But here's another thing. Lately, with so many years gone by, I am also concerned about the cultural gap which might exist between me and the potential bride. This gap could only get worse as I get older. I am too used to my lifestyle in this country while my partner might be too used to the lifestyle in India and I am not sure if I have the patience or the ability to work it all out."

"Why? Do you necessarily need to get married to an Indian woman from India? Aren't there plenty of single women here?" Lina asked.

"Yes, there are. And no, I am not fixated on just Indian women from India. I am quite open to anyone if I ever get into that situation." Even as he answered her, Rakesh looked at Lina and wondered if she had any deeper intentions behind her question, but soon dismissed it as his own imagination.

"So, there you go. You have a wide choice. Go for it and make your move," concluded Lina.

Rakesh wasn't about to surrender. He asked, "So what happens if I get married? What would you do?"

"Well, I have options, remember? I will move out and find my own housing," replied Lina.

"Is that what you really want to do?" Rakesh asked in a serious tone.

Lina looked at him, but did not answer.

~~~　　24　　~~~

Rakesh spotted them this morning – once again. He had detected a few times in the little over three months they'd lived together, but was reluctant to inquire. This time however, he decided to find out. He casually approached Lina. "Is everything alright?"

"Yeah," she dragged quizzically. "Why do you ask?"

"Your eyes are red and puffy. Is something bothering your eyes?"

"Oh. No, I am fine." Even as she replied, she turned her head away from him, avoiding eye contact with Rakesh.

"I've noticed you with puffy red eyes few times before, especially in the mornings. Is it some kind of allergy that you need to take care of, or is it something else?" Rakesh pressed on.

Lina remained quiet for a few seconds before she replied in a soft voice. "I cried last night." Before Rakesh could react, she continued, "And a few nights before."

Lina was grieving in private for her untimely loss. On several occasions, Rakesh had wondered how she coped with her loss. For the most part, with the exception of her occasional defensiveness, Lina demonstrated remarkable emotional strength. Rakesh had witnessed her complete breakdown only twice – once on the day of the tragedy, and the other during the funeral. In both instances, at the time, Lina was no more than a stranger, and Rakesh had managed to walk away from her emotions and circumstances, despite his intrigue. In the time he knew her since, Rakesh failed to discover signs of open grief with the exception of her suspicious puffy eyes. He finally realized that her private letting of tears helped her cope in public. This time, he refused to walk away. He was now involved in the lives of Lina and Madeline and therefore obliged to care for their well-being.

"Talk to me." Rakesh said, as he paved an open ended path for a conversation. Lina sat down on the couch, but remained quiet and somber.

Rakesh insisted. "I think it would help to talk out whatever is bothering you. It might help bring some kind of closure."

"I miss Brian and Makie. I miss them terribly." Lina said slowly. "I get these dreams, and they are in them. I then wake up and end up crying. The day of the shooting goes through my mind over and over again; the whole thing begins with Makie heading off to school as she did every day. I keep asking myself if there were any excuses or reasons which would have kept Makie home that day, but can't come up with one. I mean, the day was normal. Makie went to school; Brian had a short day, so he dropped Madeline off at the daycare, and I went to work. I didn't find anything abnormal; absolutely no hint of the disaster that was to occur hours later."

Rakesh sat beside her and put his arms around her shoulders. He no longer felt awkward by her closeness. He said, "I realize none of us can change the past, but I'd like you to understand one thing. Unless you choose to walk away from here on your own, you and Madeline are a part of this household, and in many ways than not, as you have already said before, are part of my life and routine as well. Which means I'd rather you not suffer through anything by yourself. So, anytime you find yourself down, let's talk. I might be able to offer words to ease your pain. If not, you'll at least get the consolation of sharing your pain with someone and not keeping them lidded within you."

Lina nodded her head in silence.

"Are you getting these dreams too often?" Rakesh asked.

"Well, sort of. I mean, for the most part, I am alright. Only when I am alone and not distracted enough, I end up with a hard time."

"Do you think consulting a psychiatrist or a counselor might help?"

"I am not sure. Should I try?"

"To be honest, I am not sure either. How about if you wait another month or so and find out how things pan out? In the meantime, don't forget to use me to share anything that's troubling you."

"Uh-huh."

"Well, let me ask you this. Are there any specific triggers which bring back your memories?"

"Uh, I haven't kept track. It's usually when I am alone. That's about all I am sure of for the moment."

"Were there any neighbors or friends in this area whom you could rely on after the shooting?"

"Not really. We didn't live in the neighborhood for too long and never made any real close contact with anyone. We spoke with a couple of neighbors when we spent time in the yard and got to know them a little bit. They happened to be among the few at the funeral. I guess our lives were too nomadic at every city we lived; we either didn't have time or put in the efforts to make lasting friends. But lately, I've managed to keep in regular touch with a few, especially with those who helped me on the day of the shooting."

"Hmm. Do you know something that I thought was unusual? The funeral at a crematorium. Why did you choose cremation over burial?"

Lina sighed. "It was cheaper. I couldn't afford a traditional funeral."

"I am sorry. Are you ok with me asking all these questions?"

"No, that's fine. Perhaps I should talk through and let them all out."

"Wouldn't hurt to do so. Anyway, after the funeral, you had the ashes collected in two separate urns. What did you do with them?"

"I left them in storage. I wasn't sure how you would react if I bring them here."

"Look, I've told you, this is now your home too and you are free to do anything you please. So, if you'd like to bring the urns, you are more than welcome to do so."

"Thanks. I'll think about it. I am not sure if that would help me heal or trigger more memories."

"On another note, if you would like to keep any pictures of your family or anyone else, don't hesitate to bring them from the storage."

"Ok."

"Before you moved here, did you take time to go through all your belongings?"

"No, I didn't get any time. I was busy with work, Madeline, and other chores."

"Tell you what. You should go to the storage one weekend and spend as much time as you need and go through all the stuff. You can decide if you want to bring anything home. I'll keep Madeline with me, so that you get enough time to look through and decide. I might be talking some gibberish, but I somehow think you can bring a reasonable closure to your loss. Better yet, we can both take a day off from work, leave Madeline at the daycare, and spend time together at the storage, just the two of us. What do you think?"

Lina stared at him in deep thought. Finally she said, "I agree. It sounds like a good idea. I also like the idea of you coming with me. Let's go next weekend. Would that be alright?"

"Absolutely," replied Rakesh.

~~~ 25 ~~~

Along the northeastern section of the condominium complex ran a walking trail which led to the Dominion Park. Despite the fact that there was nothing in particular to boast about a park which was right smack in the middle of an urban landscape, it offered a certain amount of respite for those urban dwellers who sought refuge at the relative quiet and tranquility. The summer had recently arrived. One evening, Lina and Rakesh were out for a walk at the park with Madeline. The day was pleasant with the temperature in the lower seventies; a gentle breeze blew, and the sky was void of clouds. The daylight extended well into the late evening and the residents of the condo certainly took advantage spending time outdoors. The park had few charcoal grill stands and a few benches were scattered among the trees. Two or three groups of people were grilling something which smelled delicious, enough to trigger Rakesh's appetite. Madeline ran around the open space, and played in the dirt and the grass. After a while of strolling around the park grounds, Lina and Rakesh settled down on one of the benches while Madeline continued to play.

"My parents are visiting me this year." Rakesh said, as they relaxed on the bench.

"Wow, wonderful! When are they coming?" Lina asked.

"They are working on their itinerary for a trip sometime around the end of summer. They want to leave before the weather gets cold."

"How long are they planning on staying here?"

"A couple of months or so."

"Couple of months! For that long?"

"Yeah, it's quite normal since they wouldn't be able to visit too often."

"Have they been here before?"

"Yeah, once, a long time ago, soon after I graduated. That was their first trip and we did what most family visitors tend to do – travel and visit as many tourist traps one can visit."

"So, I am assuming they will stay with you in the condo."

"Of course." Rakesh said.

"Are they aware of the living arrangement you have gotten yourself into?"

"Yes, they do. Somehow, I suspect their sudden decision to pay me a visit is in part because of my current living arrangement."

"Why do you say so?"

"Well, for one, they weren't exactly thrilled about who I was living with, to say the least."

Lina chuckled with a teasing expression. "But doesn't your mom want to eventually hook you up with a girl?"

"Of course, but you don't quite fit the bill of the kind of girl she has in her mind."

Lina laughed. "So, when did you tell them about us?"

"Uh, I think sometime shortly after you both moved in. They were in complete disbelief. Then they shot a barrage of questions. The more I explained the details, the less they were pleased. After a lengthy interrogation, they went off on an all-out offensive about how I have lost my mind, what I am doing is not good for the family, and so on and so forth. They went on and on for a while. Finally, after a whole lot of back and forth conversation, they flat out told me that it was unacceptable for me to do such a thing, and they expect me to fix the situation right away."

Lina looked hard at Rakesh and asked, "When exactly did you tell your parents about me?"

"I just told you. Soon after you moved in, uh, let me think, sometime in March. What's the matter?"

"Nothing, I am simply curious. Clearly your parents are displeased and want you to fix the situation which you haven't so far." She paused. "What did they mean by that, anyway?"

"Mean by what?"

"Fixing the situation."

"Well, from how they said it, I believe they want you both gone."

"Just like that, huh?" Lina seemed irritated.

Rakesh sensed her irritability. "Lina, easy now. I am having a conversation with you and sharing some information. Just because they say something doesn't mean I agree or will follow through their orders."

"Ok, fair enough, but you said they are visiting you soon and they are staying with you for two months. How's that going to work? What does that mean for me and Madie?"

"This is why I am having this conversation so that you are aware of what my parents are thinking and telling me. In the meantime, nothing is going to change for you and Madie, and I'll make sure of that. My parents need to find out for themselves who you are and what the living arrangement looks like. I am hoping they'll one day come to terms with it, but I am quite sure it won't be easy or quick for them. For all I know, they may never come to terms at all."

"I am not sure Rakesh. Your parents, if what you are saying is true, hold high hopes and want to get you married to some wonderful Indian bride and live a life which, in their mind, is culturally appropriate. Instead, they find you living a dysfunctional lifestyle. Until they show up here, they can only imagine how you are living. The moment they are here, they can see everything, and that's going to cause a deadly amount of additional disappointment for them. Besides, I have no desire to take any more crap from anyone, if you understand what I mean. I can only hope an abundant language barrier stands between me and your parents which would help avoid any confrontation. Any way I look, I am afraid, by the time your parents are ready to return to India, it's all going to end up in one hell of a nasty spat."

Rakesh said, "What you are saying is one hundred percent possible. But, they could also experience a change of heart once they observe how things are. I don't know yet. They are good people Lina. They are just set in their own ways as we all are. Also, their life experience outside of India is close to none, and therefore their only benchmark of life is what they know and have known in their entire life. Everything they hear and learn over the phone about me, you, and Madeline is completely strange or unknown to them. Don't you think it's very normal to be wary of the unknown? They are, and they have expressed their wariness in the form of both disappointment and an all-out offensive. Which is why I think their visit might give them the chance to experience, listen, and digest the happenings in this household. Maybe, once they get to understand the circumstances, they'll be okay. At least, that's what I am hoping would happen."

Lina was unconvinced. She felt that his parents would be more than capable of diagnosing the relationship which existed among the three. It was a relationship which began with a strange hand written note from Rakesh, and rapidly strengthened to what it was today – within a relatively short period of time. Yet, they would also be able to decipher the boundaries of their relationship. Consequently, she believed that his parents would view her and Madeline as a serious obstruction, one which would, to a significant extent, hinder their ability to place Rakesh as a son worthy of praises among the society in their homeland. Her belief was strengthened by the precedence which already existed in her own life. After all, her father held an almost identical notion.

~~~   26   ~~~

The lives and routine of Lina and Rakesh settled into a certain trajectory following a rapid, but dynamic progression of their relationship with one another, and with Madeline. In its current state, each assumed specific household roles and relied upon one another to accomplish the day to day tasks. They chose a path of interdependence despite the fact that they were individuals free of commitments to each other.

In one such sign of their ever strengthening relationship, Lina found herself able to trust Rakesh in entirety.

In the months that she knew him, Lina fluctuated between trust and doubt. Her trust allowed her to move into Rakesh's condo, while her doubt prevented her from letting the guard down, especially, in matters related to Madeline. While she always appreciated the hope that Rakesh infused into what she considered her second phase of life, she also, on occasion, experienced an overwhelming spell of mistrust. Consequently, Lina felt compelled to leave ample bread crumbs; she took that decision on the day when she contacted Rakesh for the first time, over the phone, in early December, in response to his note. Her first breadcrumb was to notify Mrs. Hamilton, the Principal of Hadley Lyons Elementary, of her phone conversation with Rakesh. Later, she got in touch with Trooper McDougall, the State Police officer who was with her on the day of the shooting, and discussed about her communication with Rakesh. Over time, she ensured to leave information of her whereabouts with her supervisor at work, couple of co-workers, and few others. She also made sure that every one of them heard from her on a regular basis. Needless to say, Rakesh was oblivious of Lina's cautionary steps. In the end however, he turned out to be a harmless person.

Now, with Lina being able to trust him, she took the first step and allowed Rakesh to be Madeline's authorized pickup from her daycare.

This permitted Lina to squeeze out few precious days to spend time on her own while Rakesh played the role of the primary caregiver.

Lina became the chef of the household. It was not entirely by choice, but more out of concern that she and Madeline might end up thriving on frozen selections. She managed the culinary environment by preparing simple and easy to make dishes while keeping Rakesh at bay from the frozen diet that he was accustomed to for numerous years. From that perspective, she took not-so-subtle control over what entered the premises of the kitchen. Fed with the far better cuisine, Rakesh went along with Lina's choices without any protest.

Rakesh on the other hand assumed the role of the household accountant. He enjoyed being one and excelled at it. Besides, he had won the confidence of Lina during his several trips to her home to help settle her bills and debt. It only seemed natural for Lina to let him manage the financial aspects of the household. In the beginning, Rakesh waited for Lina to open up her bills, or anything which pertained to a financial matter; he remembered her warning not to meddle with or pay her bills. Of late, however, he took the liberty of opening her mail and settling whatever needed to be settled. He proposed numerous changes to her financial accounts and went ahead with the implementation. He also encouraged her into a habit of disciplined long-term savings and investments. During occasions when she seemed indifferent, he made the decision for her and made sure Lina had a path set for a comfortable retirement future. Lina, for her part, consented with Rakesh's decision making.

Rakesh's life transformed to that of a family man while Lina regained a sense of normalcy which was otherwise devastatingly disrupted with the deaths of Brian and Makenzie. Over time, Rakesh and Lina fell into the habit of consulting each other anytime something of significance had to be decided upon, or if any pressing matter had to be dealt with. Each became the check and balance for the other. In another change, in the past, Rakesh had been able and willing to visit someone at a moment's notice, but lately, it became ever more common for him to decline an invitation under the pretext of an enduring commitment at home.

Madeline, the bright and lively little girl, continued her upward swing in her bonding with Rakesh. She kept him amused and he kept her entertained. Rakesh committed himself to caring for her while instilling traits of positive behavior. Lina did not mind when Rakesh deployed stern words when Madeline misbehaved. Rakesh acted every bit a parent. As a result, his relationship with Madeline had a profound effect. He found Madeline, to an increasing extent, addressing him as "Da-da". He had caught her uttering on a few occasions in the past, but had dismissed them as a slip of the tongue from a child who was still building the basic skills of vocabulary. Now, he realized that Madeline was intentionally addressing him as 'Dad', and with a conscious effort. Lina noted as well. This inevitably created minor awkward moments. However, both Lina and Rakesh did not prevent Madeline from calling him 'Dad'; they weren't sure how to get the child to comprehend the prevailing household arrangement. Besides, both adults didn't mind, especially Rakesh, who deep inside, enjoyed being addressed as 'Dad'.

Consequently, whether Rakesh came to a realization or not, it became abundantly evident that he was living the very lifestyle he chose not to. Furthermore, the transformation to his current lifestyle took no more than a few months.

Despite all these, from at least the legal angle, the underlying fact remained unchanged. Lina and Rakesh were roommates and nothing more. They each had their own rooms, their privacy, and their entitlement to pursue whatever they wished. There were a number of occasions when each privately contemplated the nature of the existing arrangement, and wondered what the future held, but neither Rakesh nor Lina had the persuasion to put their thoughts into a viable conversation, and as a result, both remained content with the status quo.

Adding to that mix was the imminent visit by Rakesh's parents. Inevitably, his parents would scrutinize the dynamics of the co-habitation and the prevailing relationship. That meant, there was a strong possibility wherein Lina and Rakesh would be forced to step out of their contentedness in order to dissect the inner meaning of their existing relationship, and determine what, if any, needed done to chart a course for the future.

~~~   27   ~~~

Lufthansa flight 757 thundered down the runway at Mumbai's Chatrapati Shivaji International Airport and climbed into the humid darkness during the wee hour of 2.55 am on a Friday in early August. The flight path of the Boeing 747-400 aircraft would take the passengers out of India and over the Arabian Sea just south of Pakistan before flying over Iran, Iraq, and Turkey. The flight would then continue over several European countries including, Bulgaria, Romania, Serbia, Hungary, and Austria before arriving in Frankfurt around eight in the morning.

Rakesh's parents were already exhausted, having lost much of their bedtime while they meandered through the rigor of the airport procedures at Mumbai - rigor which consumed most of the three hours, the minimum amount of time required of the passengers departing to international destinations. The airport went through multiple facelifts to meet the demands of the ever growing number of passengers. Consequently, there seemed to be a never ending construction and upgrades which resulted in either an improvement or a degradation of passenger facilities including the mysterious disappearances of vendors along the terminal concourses. As a result, someone who traveled through the airport even a few months ago could not rely on availing the same services which they might have experienced earlier.

The sixty-eight year old Dalpat Jaiteley and the sixty-four year old Karuna Jaiteley – Rakesh's father and mother, respectively – were scheduled to arrive into Detroit Metropolitan Wayne County Airport just before five pm on Friday after a six-hour layover in Frankfurt.

Rakesh left work early and headed to the airport; he hoped not to get paralyzed in the peak hour traffic on the freeways leading to the airport. By the time he arrived at the International Arrivals in the North Terminal, the time was almost five. According to the arrivals status board, Lufthansa flight 442 from Frankfurt had landed. After another ninety minutes, his parents walked out through the security doors.

During the drive from the airport to the condo, Rakesh's mother embarked on a monologue of their experience of the past several hours. She elaborated on the quirks at Mumbai airport, the strange tastes of the food on Lufthansa, the inevitable jet lag, the notoriously confusing layout at Frankfurt airport - although she stated it was better than Charles De Gaulle in Paris where they had the layover during their first trip to the USA, the long walk between the gates at Frankfurt, the long layover in Germany, the long wait at the US Immigration, the lengthy questions by the Customs and Border Protection officer, and so on. Rakesh listened to his mother's narration in silence. Meanwhile, Rakesh's father was fast asleep in the car.

As they neared the condo, the conversation switched from that of the flight to one of far more importance to Rakesh's mother.

"Is that American girl still living in your house?" His mother asked.

"Of course she is. I've told you that all along, and please, she has a name. I'd like you to address her as Lina and not as the 'American girl'," replied Rakesh in as much of a neutral tone he could muster.

Karuna Jaiteley said nothing, and her silence pretty much summarized her continuing disapproval of her son's choice of lifestyle.

After a momentary silence, she asked, "Did you call Mehra Uncle?"

"Who?"

"This is exactly what bothers me, Rakesh. I keep telling you all the time and you don't listen. You should keep in touch with our people."

"Ma, I don't even know who you are talking about. Who is this Mehra Uncle?"

"He is the well-to-do Doctor who lives in Detroit. I told you about him on the phone a month ago. He lives in, what's the place called? Chelsea, I think. Isn't that Detroit?"

"Alright, well, I don't remember, and I don't have his number. Chelsea is about an hour west from where I live. Anyway, how do you know him?"

"His brother and your father have known each other for many years. Mehra has a daughter and they have shown interest in you for their daughter. You should call them right away and invite them so that you can meet their daughter while we are here. In that way, we'll get to meet her as well. She is a US citizen."

Rakesh muttered something under his breath and the wind noise in the car helped protect him from being heard. So, here they were – his parents – who somehow managed to find someone in his vicinity. Rakesh wondered if he had this girl's photo by any chance.

"Let me think about it," replied Rakesh in a non-committal manner. He pondered the entire scene - him, his parents, the Mehras and their daughter aka the yet-another-promising-bride, Lina and Madeline – all in the same abode at the same time. He wondered how the entire thing would play out. Maybe, he thought, this could be a wonderful case study to check out everyone's reaction and utilize this opportunity to put things to rest. In any event, one thing remained certain; it wasn't bound to be a pleasant or a comfortable get together.

Mrs. Jaiteley broke the ten second silence. "What do you mean you'll think about it? I will speak to Mehra and arrange a day for all of us to meet. Also, one more thing. It won't be appropriate for that American girl, uh, I mean Lina, and her child to be in the house when we all meet. I don't want Mehra's family to think badly of us. So, you should tell Lina in advance so that she can make arrangements to be away for a while."

Well, so that was how his mom planned on solving the dilemma, thought Rakesh. Simply get rid of Lina and Madeline 'for a while'. Also, by some convoluted means, Lina was an American girl while Mehra's US born daughter received the status of 'our people', despite the US citizenship. Rakesh became irritated and his patience wore thin. Yet, he kept his calm and said, "Ma, first of all, let me think about it. You can't just force me to invite someone. Second, even if we have them over, I don't want you to raise their hopes, because I am not going to commit anything to anybody. Finally, Lina and Madeline live in this home. It is theirs as much as it is mine. I will not tell her to leave just because you think it is inappropriate. That is plain rude."

His mom interrupted him. "Then, we'll need to arrange to meet at Mehra's house."

Rakesh replied, "If it is your desire to meet with Mehra and family, so be it. I don't care where we meet. But, I will make sure they are aware, and understand my current living arrangements with Lina and Madeline."

"Don't be crazy. What will they think if they know what you are doing? I don't want you to tell them anything."

"What do you think I am doing?" Rakesh retorted. "I've explained to you before. I made a commitment to Lina on certain things, and I will keep up my words. That is not going to change, and I really don't care what anyone thinks. So, you can make me meet with anyone you like, but the only way this is going to work is by letting them all know about my current situation and get them to deal with it."

Karuna Jaiteley was completely taken aback, but she finally quieted down, more out of exhaustion after the long flight. Rakesh wondered how the next two months would pan out with his parents. His dad meanwhile remained fast asleep.

Lina and Madeline were home when Rakesh and his parents walked in. Madeline, as she always did, rushed toward Rakesh, and held her arms up, urging him to pick her up, which Rakesh gladly did. As soon as Madeline saw Rakesh's parents, she instinctively reacted to the two new faces - she threw her arms around Rakesh's neck and held him tight. This was duly noted by the Jaiteleys with a mix of disappointment, scorn, and alarm. The Jaiteleys weren't prepared to witness the all too obvious parental level bond which prevailed between Rakesh and Madeline. Rakesh introduced his parents to Madeline and urged the little girl to say hello to them. She just waved her hands with a shy smile. His parents returned her greetings with a wary nod. Rakesh then introduced Lina who said hello with a cautious optimism. She received the same wary nod in return. Both Rakesh and Lina hoped for an improved interaction with the Jaiteleys once they've had a good night's sleep and recovered from the exhaustion of the long trip.

The weekend served as the beginning and one of many ample opportunities for the Jaiteleys to witness and take note of the inner workings of the household. Lina prepared breakfast - a combination of pancakes, poached eggs, toast and fruits. For the Jaiteleys, none classified as authentic Indian cuisine. Rakesh had anticipated the culinary troubles ahead of time and had prepared a concoction from frozen ready-to-eat packages. He had also stocked the refrigerator with 'homemade' rotis bought at BAGS – the Asian grocery store. His parents were glad to have that for breakfast, although they objected to eating processed food – something Lina agreed. Rakesh's mother declared that she would cook fresh and palatable Indian meals as long as they stayed in the USA. However, few of the contents in the refrigerator and the freezer perplexed his mother, as the appliance held 'his', 'hers', and 'their' food items. Beyond the chicken, strange packages of meat lay in the freezer. Rakesh described the items - beef, pork and turkey; meat his parents had never eaten in their lives. His mom once again exuded disappointment at what she viewed as Rakesh's complete disregard of traditions. The Jaiteleys watched Rakesh feed, bathe, and clothe Madeline. They took note of the level of engagement that Rakesh had with Madeline. They were caught in a bind. They had a strong urge to limit Rakesh's interaction with Madeline who, in their mind, was a stranger's child; however an instinctive affinity toward an adorable little child prevented them from doing so. They also found relief when they confirmed with their own eyes that Lina and Rakesh had their own separate bedrooms, although his parents were fully aware that this was not adequate to prevent their son from engaging in anything they considered inappropriate.

They witnessed several private conversations between Lina and Rakesh. In a number of instances, they pressed Rakesh to divulge the content and context of those conversations, and almost always, he casually waved them off stating, "It's nothing." The gesture and the response irritated his mother more than it did his father. One time, around the kitchen sink, while Rakesh and Lina shared the chores, he muttered something to her, and she giggled and playfully pushed him by his shoulders. Rakesh's mother considered that as a completely inappropriate behavior on Lina's part.

One day, everyone went as a group for shopping and other errands. At every location, regardless of who the item was purchased for, Rakesh paid the bill. His parents became amply concerned that Lina was taking advantage of Rakesh. Lina attempted simple conversations with the Jaiteleys; she succeeded sometimes and failed many more times. Their responses remained to the point and detached. Lina wasn't sure if that was due to the language barrier or their dislike toward her. She eventually concluded that it was due to their indifference to her. Lina made every attempt to ensure that Rakesh's parents were comfortable around the house; she did and offered what she believed to be a gesture of hospitality. Every bit was instead scrutinized and judged. It didn't take long for Lina to realize that she was being constantly monitored and evaluated. Despite that, Lina kept reminding herself that it could be just a matter of few more days before the Jaiteleys would warm up to her.

In another effort to thaw the apparent deep freeze, Lina decided to adopt a different approach. She decided to prepare some Indian dessert. After a mental browsing of her list of desserts she had recently learned to make, Lina prepared mango Kulfi with a topping of chopped strawberries. Rakesh's dad immensely enjoyed Lina's meticulous preparation of the Kulfi and finally voiced his opinion with praises. However, Rakesh's mother maintained her detached attitude. Lina was pleased to have at least one barrier broken down, one tiny step.

As a matter of routine, after Madeline went to bed, Lina and Rakesh spent time together to reflect upon the musings of their day, discuss issues, resolve predicaments, or simply watch TV in silence. This time however, the Jaiteleys were around. As always, Lina made herself a cup of hot chocolate, and offered to make espresso for Rakesh's parents. She settled down on the couch with her beverage, next to

Rakesh as she did all the time. This time around, Rakesh's parents happened to be the ones who found Lina's nearness to their son discomforting.

In the end, the Jaiteleys summarized their keen observations in a manner they saw fit. What they concluded was an existence of a close, if not intimate, relationship between Lina and Rakesh, with a young child added to the mix – a child not of Rakesh's blood. They had hoped, wished, and dreamed of Rakesh being married to an Indian girl who was on par with their family status. They had hoped for a grandchild bore out of their heritage. Instead, what they found was an unmarried relationship between their son and an American girl who shared nothing in common with them. Adding to the insult was the presence of a toddler who treated Rakesh as her father, and yet, they could not accept the child as their grandchild. This terrible disappointment served as a powerful catalyst for Rakesh's mother to hasten the meeting with the Mehras.

~~~   28   ~~~

The 'well-to-do Doctor' - the 'Mehra Uncle' - was Dr. Pratap Mehra, a neurosurgeon who practiced at a major hospital in the metro area. His wife, Shabna Mehra, a homemaker now, used to be a practicing physician in India before the couple immigrated to the US numerous years ago. Their unmarried daughter, the one being proposed for Rakesh, was Darya Mehra. Darya had two older brothers, both medical doctors, living and practicing in rural regions of Michigan. Darya rebelled and refused to follow the family profession. She also decided to live as far away as possible from the rest of her family, and as a result lived in California and worked as a successful 'Freelance Animator'.

Darya's job title underestimated what she actually did. Her work formed the critical foundation of any modern animation movie, something far more than simple animation. The movie studios hired her to be part of the storyboarding team. Storyboarding formed an essential stage of the animation process which helped develop the storyline. Storyboarding comprised of drawings similar to that of a comic strip which helped the entire team understand the sequence of the movie. This, in turn, served as a foundational template to revert and refer back during other stages of the movie production. The work stayed exciting and involved unlimited imaginative freedom, resulting in Darya cherishing her career.

Rakesh's mother, Karuna Jaiteley took charge of the entire planning of the meeting with the Mehras. In a twist of events, the day of the get together, scheduled for a weekend two weeks away, was decided to be held at Rakesh's condo. Rakesh, for his part, gave adequate heads-up to Lina about the entire upcoming event, and prepped her for any possible turn in the wrong direction. Lina had no clue about the protocol of the get together, but was excited to take on the role of the observer even as she felt apprehensive of the outcome. Darya was flying in from California for the weekend event. Rakesh was not sure on how much say

Darya had in the whole matter.

Few days prior to the planned event, Rakesh asked if Lina would be interested in wearing Indian attire during the gathering. Lina, clueless but curious, agreed. She asked what he had in mind and he admitted he had no clue as well. However, they fired up the internet and did an exhaustive search for the appropriate attire. Eventually, Lina pointed to something which piqued her interest; it was a Lehenga Choli. After several more minutes of searching through the vast collection of Lehengas, Rakesh suggested a burnt orange embroidered Lehenga piece. He added that the color of the clothing would match with her hazel and brown heterochromatic eyes. Lina agreed, and Rakesh placed the online order. The Lehenga arrived by UPS five days later.

On the Saturday of the get together, Rakesh's mother was both excited and flustered. The fanfare began bright and early on Saturday. Mrs. Jaiteley embarked on a cooking spree of an array of sweet, spicy, and aromatic food. She dispatched Rakesh multiple times to fetch the appropriate ingredients from Badsha Asian Groceries. At some point during the day, Lina took pity on Rakesh and ended up running the errand a couple of times. By mid-afternoon, the kitchen filled up with ample variety of fresh homemade food, most of which Lina barely recognized. Once the cooking and other activities came to a completion, Rakesh's mother went around, inspected, and re-inspected everything she had arranged – food, decorations, few holy items, and Rakesh's attitude.

Mrs. Jaiteley was completely displeased at the fact that Lina and Madeline would remain in the house when the guests arrived. Adding to her chagrin was the knowledge that Lina would be wearing a Lehenga. She viewed the choice of clothing as Lina's not-so-veiled attempt to compete with Darya. The fact that it was Rakesh who suggested the Lehenga was lost on Mrs. Jaiteley, despite Rakesh's emphasis on the same.

As a result, she took every opportunity to express her displeasure to her husband and son. She even recommended that Rakesh not hold or play with Madeline while the guests were present. Trying to explain Rakesh's living arrangements with an American woman and her child was horrifying enough; she had no appetite to explain the close bond between Rakesh and the child. Rakesh, on the other hand, remained stubborn and did not budge neither on her displeasure nor her recommendations. Meanwhile, Rakesh's father seemed caught in the middle between his stubborn son and his frustrated wife.

The Mehra family arrived a few minutes past five in the evening.

Darya adorned a white and maroon cotton silk printed Churidar Kameez which carried an intricate floral pattern. She wore a matching maroon shade stone studded earrings. She had a rich, dark, long flowing hair, and a dimpled smile. At thirty four years old, inevitably, she also endured her parents' concern of remaining unmarried ever since she turned twenty five. In all aspects, Darya was an attractive woman. In the eyes of Rakesh's mother, she was the perfect woman and bride – beautiful, educated, and an employed professional, not to mention a fellow Indian from a known family at an appropriate and perfect age for Rakesh.

The customary greetings were exchanged. Everyone introduced everyone else. Lina and Madeline were left out in the frenzy. Once the fervor of introductions ebbed, Rakesh stepped in and introduced Lina to the Mehras. Meanwhile, Madeline had made Rakesh pick her up and was now clinging to him tightly. Mrs. Jaiteley became restless with rising anxiety. Rakesh's mother had not informed the Mehras about Lina and the little girl; in her mind, she found no need for it. Consequently, the Mehra family members were highly curious, if not anything else, of Lina and Madeline's presence. The curiosity only escalated at the sight of Madeline holding Rakesh in a firm grip.

The conversation among the Mehras and the Jaiteleys drifted from one random topic to another in no particular order. Rakesh and Darya spoke little to none with seemingly limited opportunity to utter anything which their parents would consider worthwhile. After a while, Madeline got bored and deserted the group in order to play with her stuff. Lina sat quietly as well, understanding very little to none of what was being said, as most of the conversation occurred in Hindi with random sprinkle of English in between words. A few minutes later, Rakesh's mother scurried into the kitchen and brought the first round of eatables. This was followed by a number of arbitrary queries targeted at either Rakesh or Darya by the other's parents. This happened to be the parents' attempt to understand the personalities of their potential future son- or daughter-in-law. It was an organized and amicable interrogation. After about half-hour, Rakesh became thoroughly bored, and he drifted toward the middle distance as he tuned out the conversations. That's when he heard Darya ask him something. He jolted out of his self-oblivion.

"I am sorry, what?" Rakesh asked.

"How do you know each other?" Darya asked Rakesh again, with a pleasant dimpled smile, pointing at Lina.

Lina sat up straight and geared for what could potentially become the most interesting evening. Karuna Jaiteley fidgeted on the couch uncomfortably. Dalpat Jaiteley simply looked around, trying to ignore the awkwardness threatening to settle in soon. Pratap and Shabna Mehra - Darya's parents - were relieved that they were not the ones forced to ask that question; nevertheless were eager to find the answer.

"Oh, Lina is a friend of mine, and Madeline is her daughter. They…"

Darya interrupted. She looked at Lina and said, "I see. By the way, you look very beautiful in the Lehenga. From where did you buy this?"

"Thanks." Lina replied. "We searched and found it online. I don't recall the name of the seller."

"Do you live close by?" Darya asked, intrigued at Lina's reference of 'we'.

"No, we live here with Rakesh." Lina replied.

"Excuse me?" Darya bore a startled expression.

"This is only a temporary thing." Rakesh's mother blurted in a haste.

"What do you mean you live with Rakesh? Dalpat, what's going on?" Darya's father asked, sounding concerned.

Rakesh quickly jumped in. "Lina and Madeline live here. This is their home as well and it is definitely not a temporary thing." Rakesh said looking at his mother and emphasizing the phrase 'not a temporary thing'.

Darya's parents were increasingly confused. "Dalpat, what is this? How come you never told us about this? Rakesh, what is your relationship with her?" Darya's father asked, pointing at Lina and Rakesh.

Before Rakesh's father uttered a word, his mom stirred up further confusion in an effort to temper down what was heading in the wrong path.

"Rakesh has no relationship with the American girl. We are very much interested only in Darya. You see…."

Rakesh quickly interrupted his mother.

"Ma, can you please quiet down? Let me talk. Darya and her parents have every right to know what's going on here."

Taken aback by Rakesh's authoritative voice, the group quieted to hear him more.

Rakesh began to explain. "Last October, a shooting occurred at one of the Beniton Heights elementary schools. Does anyone remember?"

Darya and her parents nodded yes.

"Lina's husband, Brian, and their older daughter, Makenzie, who was in kindergarten, were killed in that shooting."

Darya had a shocked expression on her face and her palm covered her mouth. Lina looked down on the floor.

Rakesh continued, "Makenzie's teacher, Karen Wharton, lost her life too. Karen was the wife of my friend and ex-coworker, John. John was out of town on business, so I went to the school to track down Karen and her two boys. That's when I came across Lina. I didn't know her at the time; I just happened to notice her in the area where we were all gathered. Anyway, one thing led to another and we met at a later time in the library. There were several things we spoke about and, uh, I am not going to discuss any personal details, but we made a combined decision that it would be a workable option for her and Madeline to live here in this home. So, here we are."

After an awkward moment of silence, Darya spoke first. "Lina, I am so sorry for your loss. I hope you are able to move on, and wish you the best."

Lina said, "Thanks Darya." She added, "Rakesh has been of immense help. You folks have no idea how difficult it would have been if I had to manage everything that I had to, all by myself."

Rakesh then continued, "There is nothing going on between us other than being good friends and living together. And I've already explained why she is living here. I also want to make it clear to you three," he said pointing to the Mehras, "you are here because my mother insisted that I meet Darya. I am not interested in any form of marriage alliance with your family. I never did. My mother in fact wanted Lina and Madeline out of the house while you are all here. I refused. The only thing I agreed to, more to appease my mother than anything else, and will ever agree, is to meet anyone on the condition that they are aware of my living arrangements. That way, they can hear my story and we can then let the chips fall wherever it may."

After a pause, Rakesh went on, "So, you or anyone else can continue to express interest in me; however, I need to see a concrete, workable solution for Lina and Madeline which will assure them a safety net. I will not negotiate or compromise on that front. And there is yet another thing. As much as it may sound awkward, Madeline treats me as her dad and has even started addressing me as her dad. Trust me, this has put me, and I am sure Lina as well, in a bind, but I will not abandon Madeline. I am fully aware that my mother is utterly displeased at my current situation, but I made a commitment, more of an offer, to Lina when I was at her husband's funeral, and there is no way I will go back on that commitment."

Rakesh then addressed his parents, specifically his mother. "I have told you about Lina and Madeline, and tried to reason with you ever since they moved here. I also stated that I will bring this up if and when anyone shows up at my doorstep with a potential bride in their hands. Yet, as in many other cases, you insisted on not disclosing this to the Mehras. You cannot force me into a future with the intention of making my current or past somehow vanish into thin air. Lina and Madeline are not some casual fling. I can't simply throw them out the door so we all can pretend to protect our so called status, pride, and Indian traditions. They are real people who have been impacted by a loss, and I will stand by them to the best of my ability for as long as they need it."

"There is one more thing." Rakesh said, as he addressed his parents. "I realize it is difficult for you to accept what or who I am right now. But you are going to be with me for a few more weeks. Lina has made multiple attempts to break the ice between her and you two, but, so far, all I've seen from you is indifference toward her and her little girl. I'd strongly recommend that you both make the best of your stay and enjoy your time with all of us. Please try to get to know Lina and Madeline, because they are here to stay regardless of how you feel or what you think."

Not one spoke a word. Lina was duly impressed by Rakesh's speech. However, she developed a nagging concern as she was not sure what could become of their habitation arrangement as a result of the latest dynamics.

Finally, Darya's father spoke up. "Well, I guess Rakesh has spoken his mind. I am of the opinion he gets to choose his life and he has indeed chosen his path. From that point of view, I fully support him. Dalpat and Karuna, I just wish you both had told us about Lina and her child. We could have still met, but in a more different setting. So, what's next?"

Rakesh said, "Dr. Mehra, thank you for your support. It means a lot to me. Anyway, since you all are here, let's spend the time together. I'd like you all to enjoy dinner with us as planned. Darya, any objections?"

"No, none at all. We'd love to stay and get to know all of you more," replied Darya.

~~~   29   ~~~

It was the end of October and the first chill of the season began to descend into Michigan. Rakesh's parents returned home to India a week before. The remainder of their stay with Rakesh since the visit of the Mehras was mostly uneventful. Forced by the circumstances, and after many more emphatic advices from Rakesh, his parents did make an effort, albeit not a strong one, to thaw their deep freeze toward Lina. Rakesh's father demonstrated a higher level of relative openness compared to his mother. Madeline, on the other hand, was still full of innocence and did not discriminate in her show of social skills. It didn't take much for her to shed her inhibition against Rakesh's parents. Once again, forced by the child's natural behavior of bonding with them, the Jaiteleys relented and reciprocated with a positive attitude, although in a tentative manner.

About a week before they were scheduled to leave the USA, Rakesh's mother pulled him aside. "I want to ask you something."

"Uh-huh." Rakesh muttered.

"You won't get mad, will you?"

"Well, I am not sure what you are going to ask, but no, I won't get mad."

"Are you going to marry Lina?"

"What?" Rakesh was startled. His mother clearly had not given up on the idea of Rakesh being married and this question betrayed a sense of desperation on her part.

"I mean, your father and I spoke about this for a number of days. She seems to be a good girl, after all. We always hoped that you would choose someone from our community and, uh, someone who wasn't married before, but you and Lina are close to each other. We've always wanted the best for you, and if this is what you both want, we are okay as well. She will never be accepted among our relatives, but if it makes you happy, we are fine with the marriage."

Lina somehow had a charm of not being accepted among families, thought Rakesh dryly.

"Ma, I am happy to hear you say what you are saying. But listen, Lina and I have never thought about getting married to each other. She is too young for me. She's only twenty nine. In any case, I don't even know if I want to get married to her or anyone else for that matter. She still misses her husband and daughter and she needs to move past that, and I am going to support her as much as I can. Besides, I have no idea what she has in her mind."

"So, why don't you go talk to her? Maybe give her the option of getting married to you. She has known you for several months and I am sure she'll at least hear you out."

Rakesh objected. "That would be totally inappropriate. What would she think?"

"Why is it inappropriate? You both live like husband and wife right now. You care for Madeline so much. Well, at least talk to her. Find out what she has in her mind. After that, whatever happens, let it happen."

Rakesh pondered his mother's words few times after his parents left. Then he forgot about them altogether.

The Tuesday of October 29th brought a flurry of terrifying memories for Lina. It was one year to the day since the shooting occurred. On this day last year, upon getting word about the incident, she had rushed to the daycare from work, picked up Madeline, and drove to Hadley Lyons Elementary, shaken, confused, terrified, and in tears. One year to the day passed since Brian and Makenzie lost their lives due to the despicable act of a lone gunman. Rakesh sensed her disturbed state of mind right away, and found her in the same state until the end of the day. Rakesh too remembered his day with the twins, Jake and Josh. He recollected his observations of Lina, who at the time, in the eyes of Rakesh, was nothing more than a random young woman who intrigued him through her sorrow.

It only seemed like yesterday, yet a year passed with major changes in both Lina and Rakesh's life. Lina's despondence continued for the next couple of days. In a marked sign of change however, Lina no longer grieved in private or silence. She expressed herself to Rakesh. In another notable sign of change, Rakesh did not stay away as a silent and awkward spectator. As a result, she was outspoken of her thoughts, and he in return, offered the best level of support. In the end, his closeness seemed to help ease her pain of loss.

On one Friday night, the three returned home after a sumptuous dinner at the local Japanese Steakhouse. Madeline was fast asleep.

Rakesh helped put the little girl to bed. With nothing particular to do at this hour, Lina and Rakesh idled around while contemplating whether to turn on a movie or simply settle for whatever distasteful reality show that was on the TV at the moment.

"Your dad was glued quite a bit on the Animal Planet channel, wasn't he?" Lina quipped.

"Yeah, maybe that was one of the few channels where he didn't have to pay attention to anyone speaking. He could idle his brain and enjoy the show."

The conversation gradually morphed deeper about Rakesh's parents. Ever since they returned to India, both Lina and Rakesh often discussed the dynamics which prevailed during their stay. Rakesh had not brought up the conversation his mother had with him about Lina since he did not consider it appropriate; at least not yet. For Lina, her opinions about his parents were split. At times, she carried the urge to empathize with them as she witnessed their sense of urgency – or desperation – to see Rakesh married and lead a traditional life which they were accustomed to. Other times, she underwent a sense of consternation toward them. Although, they never spoke ill in front of her, Lina discerned the impenetrable, invisible wall that the Jaiteleys had erected between them and her. Rakesh's father seemed accepting of her, or at least of the prevailing circumstances, but for the most part went along with his wife in a show of solidarity. At times, he just remained neutral. Lina was sure that his parents believed her to be nothing more than an unnecessary burden which kept, and would keep Rakesh from fulfilling his parents' wishes – if Rakesh ever intended to fulfill their wishes, that is.

Rakesh carried the advantage of being able to relate to both his original culture as well as the one in which he currently lived and called home. He could therefore morph as needed to suit the needs of his parents and those of Lina's. Lina, on the other hand, had to improvise during those times when she attempted to make his parents feel as welcome as possible. In any event, she found unable to decipher their mind. In the end, at times she did her best to accommodate them, and at other times, simply gave up trying.

Amid their late night conversation which fluctuated between bursts of dialogues and prolonged silence, Lina looked straight at Rakesh and asked, "Will you be asking us to leave?"

"The what?" Rakesh asked, completely flummoxed at her question.

Lina repeated her question. Rakesh was still unclear what she was talking about and attempted to clarify. "Do you mean if I'd ask you and

Madeline to find some other place to live?"

"Yes."

"For heaven's sake, what makes you ask this question?" Rakesh sounded incredulous. He assumed that he was, without a doubt, clear with Lina – and his parents for that matter – on where he stood on this issue, but apparently not.

"Well, your parents, specifically, your mother, is hell bent on getting you married. The whole thing was quite obvious during our get together with Darya and her parents. It was obvious again by your mother's sheer indifference to me, although I might add she did seem to come around, enough for me to notice. Let's face the facts Rakesh, your parents want you to be settled and follow the tradition or cultural footsteps. I guess that's only a fair and reasonable expectation. Don't you think?"

"Yes, everything you said is true, but do you also remember my response to the entire group when my mother tried to shove the matrimonial deal with Darya down my throat?"

"Yeah, but...."

"No buts...," interrupted Rakesh. "What I said is what counts. Let me ask you something. If I do intend to get married and fly away to my new life, don't you think I will inform you way ahead of time? I am not going to disappear or kick you both out."

Lina was quiet for a moment. Rakesh wondered if this might be a good time to bring up what his mother had mentioned, and whether or not he would be able to put her fears to rest. Instead, he sat quietly hoping for Lina to break the silence.

Lina did break the silence. "I am afraid we might lose you, Rakesh. I mean, I know I have no right to stop you from pursuing your life, and I am sure I can figure things out myself and everything else in between, but, uh, I don't know, I just hate to start another path in my life once again."

Rakesh decided to reveal his mom's thought. "Alright. I am going to tell you something that I've been reluctant to share with you. Quite honestly, I have no idea whether this would make you feel better or worse."

"What is it?" Lina asked with an immense curiosity.

"A week or so before my parents left, my mother asked me if I was going to marry you."

Lina burst out giggling. "Oh my gosh, really?"

"Yeah, really."

"What in the world made her ask that?"

"Uh, I guess, it was her desperation to get me married. Well it's a combination of seeing me married and her observation of us."

"Hmm. And what were her observations?"

"Well, according to her, we are close to each other and practically behaving like a couple."

"Umm. How come she had a change of heart?"

"Well, uh, looks like my parents spoke to their hearts' content and they realized, after all, us being married to each other would not be a bad option. Of course, she made it clear that you would not be accepted within our family, society, etc., but the arrangement would be acceptable for them."

"Did you tell her that I am a veteran when it comes to not being accepted by families?" Lina asked with a playful sarcasm.

Before Rakesh could answer, Lina continued with a mischievous grin, "So, what did you tell your mother?"

"You are enjoying this, aren't you?" Rakesh asked.

"Yeah, this is fun. So, tell me what you told her."

"Well, I told her that it would be highly inappropriate for me to discuss such things with you and…"

"Whoa, wait a minute. Why do you think it is inappropriate?"

"How can it be appropriate? We happened to stumble upon each other's life through a series of events, met at midpoint, and eventually made a decision to live together. That doesn't mean I can obligate you with a proposal of marriage just because my mother thinks I am better off being married."

"Hmm. Rakesh, let's revisit what you just said. We didn't exactly stumble upon each other and 'meet at the midpoint'. You started the whole thing by writing me a note which over time led to you offering your home to us."

"And you voluntarily responded to the note and eventually took up the offer of my home – voluntarily, if I may add. So, in my opinion, we did meet at the midpoint," rebutted Rakesh.

"Alright, fair enough. Anyway, we are digressing here. I still don't understand why it is inappropriate for you to ask me what your mother wanted you to ask."

"I don't know. I find it inappropriate for me to impose on you like that, considering the circumstances and the loss you've been through."

"How do you know it is inappropriate unless you actually ask the question? I am not going to bite just because you ask. Well, I can't say I have the cleanest record on biting," she said, recalling the tussle with her father which resulted in her biting his arm, "but, you know what I am saying."

Rakesh said, "Alright, if you say so. And since you asked, let me throw this hypothetical question at you. If I indeed were to ask you if you'd marry me, what would your response be?"

"I would give your proposition a positive consideration." Lina said with a straight face and without any hesitation.

Rakesh chuckled, especially at the formality of her reply; however, upon seeing a lack of a reciprocating chuckle from Lina, he turned serious and asked, "Are you serious?"

Lina nodded in affirmative. Rakesh was stunned as he clearly did not expect Lina's response.

~~~   30   ~~~

Lina's response to Rakesh's question was not only assertive, but also opened the door to a new possibility; something Rakesh had neither seriously considered nor expected, despite his mother's goading. With Lina now out in the clear with her view point on what Rakesh treated as nothing more than hypothetical, he was instantly thrust into a situation which required serious contemplation of the path he should pursue.

"Lina, do you really mean whatever you just said?" Rakesh felt a continued sense of disbelief.

"Yes, I do. Shall we talk more about it?"

"Well, of course, we should. I am concerned quite a bit at the direction of our conversation."

"Why? All you asked me was a hypothetical question and I answered you with my perspective. Of course, the answer I gave you was well meant and not just hypothetical."

"And that's what I am concerned about."

Lina rolled her eyes. "Okay. I'll hear you out. What's the big problem?"

"I am afraid your response is premature or, uh, impulsive. What I mean is, you are probably finding a need to be attached to someone, not because of a sense of insecurity, but because of fear which makes you think you could end up alone with Madeline."

"So, except for the premature and impulsive part, what if whatever you said is true? What's wrong with that?"

"No, nothing is wrong. All I am....."

Lina interrupted. "I didn't say I wanted to get married to you; rather, I'd give your proposal a positive consideration if you were to ask me."

"Well, your response sounds like a judgment from a venture capitalist on a business proposal. Anyway, to me, what you said sounds like a yes. Listen, this is simple; I don't want you to end up with regrets.

First of all, I am not going anywhere, and I am not leaving you or Madeline. So, there is no need for you to jump into a permanent life with me. I need you to take as much time as you want in order to check out whatever's out there in the near future. You are way too young, or more appropriately, I should say, I am too old for you. You might be happy in my company now, but who knows, at a later time, you might find someone who would be a perfect fit for you. A long and bright future awaits you Lina; something you shouldn't deprive yourself. I want you to allow yourself the time to work out all of those things."

"So, what you are saying is that I could go man-hunting if I want to. Is that all?"

"Well, uh, yes, if you want to. It's not a question of whether you could; perhaps you should. You are a free person to do whatever you wish to. You are free to 'man-hunt' – as you so eloquently put it - date, marry, etc."

"What about Madeline? She looks up to you as her dad. She is attached to you. As she grows up, she most likely will not hold any memories of Brian; rather it's you who will make an impact on her life. What are you going to do about her?"

Rakesh nodded in silence before he responded. "I enjoy every bit of my time with Madeline. You know this as much as I do, and I would love to continue the same. As a matter of fact, I love your company as well. I enjoy what we three do together. I wouldn't want anything to change. My wish would be for you and Madeline to be with me permanently, but this is just my wish. I don't want my wish to come at your expense; which is why I am saying you need to allow yourself time to figure out what lay in store for the future."

"Well, it's the same here for me too, Rakesh. I enjoy your company. I cherish the fact that Madeline loves to be with you. On a more selfish note, you have brought stability to our lives which otherwise would have been who knows how. I'd rather stick to the person, someone that I know who can offer personal and financial stability for me, rather than go on a fishing expedition to find somebody else. I'd like to settle down. Losing Brian and Makie was difficult enough; I do not wish to create new problems in my life. I realize that I struggle with their memories, and on some days, those things hit me hard. I wish I was like Madeline and simply forget over time, but I most likely will never, and I'll need to live with that. I am sure I'll eventually move on; with you around, it has been far quicker. I don't want to lose any of those. That is why it scares me to think that there is a possibility - however remote it may be - where you might find your own life and move away from us."

After he listened to Lina, Rakesh offered yet another affirmation. "Well, I am going to reassure you once more and continue doing until you are convinced – I am not leaving you and Madeline."

"So, let's get this straight. You will not leave us. You love our company and you enjoy our time together. Meanwhile, I am not interested in looking for men. So, I don't want to leave either. I don't for a moment believe that I'll regret being with you. Madeline, in the meantime, is clueless on which direction she wants to go; however, she is good at one thing – she loves you unconditionally. So, tell me again, why were you concerned when I answered the way I did to your 'hypothetical question'?"

Rakesh smiled and shook his head. He realized he wasn't winning the debate.

With a purposeful effort, Lina continued her point of view. "I am not quite sure if I should, or want to marry you. I fell in love with Brian and we got married. I can't say the same now; not yet, at least. I am also aware you are a scared chicken as far as marriage goes. Your life history is a testament to that."

Rakesh laughed.

She went on. "In any case, you have stood up to most challenges and quirks every married man faces. You tolerate us without any major qualms. You may not want to be a father or a husband anytime soon, but you are already serving the role, and serving them well. That says it all, and I am extremely happy with that. So, if your parents feel that you need to be married in order to complete the perceived incompleteness in your life, I am open to the idea. I'll marry you and be with you forever. I know I will not regret whatsoever."

Rakesh was pleasantly astounded at Lina's stand. He was also delighted to hear firsthand of her trust and confidence in him on most aspects of their daily life. He said, "Thank you. That is an extremely gracious offer on your part. But you don't have to marry me because of my parents. Don't worry about them. If they were able to - in two or so months - turn around and find the strength to envision us as a married couple, I am sure they'll come to terms and accept us the way we are and the choices we make from now on."

"So, what is the final decision?" Lina had a sweet smile as she sought to put this issue to rest.

"Well, I guess it's settled. Let's continue our lives together the way we've been for the past few months. Let's take one beautiful day at a time. What do you say?"

"I can certainly live with that. I agree." Lina's response demonstrated emphatic finality.

Rakesh then asked, "On another note, have you considered getting in touch with your mother at least, and perhaps make amends?"

"Well, the thought has crossed my mind, but I am not going to rush into anything. Not yet. I'll think carefully before I make any move." Lina was in no hurry to rekindle the past after being through numerous eventful years.

A few seconds passed as Rakesh considered her words in silence. He then stood up from the couch, walked over to the window which partly faced the woods of the condo's common area, and parted the blinds. The season's first snow had fallen and the ground was covered with a thin but fresh coat of snow, punctured only by the markings of the nocturnal critters. The moon peered out from behind the clouds to light the night sky. As Rakesh glanced out the window in preoccupied silence, Lina walked over and stood next to Rakesh. She looked at the clearing skies and the bright moonlight.

Rakesh turned and looked at Lina. He then stepped closer, placed one arm around her, and nudged her closer to him. As she moved closer and met her eyes with his, he put his other arm around her in an embrace. He then remarked, "Have I mentioned this before? You have very beautiful eyes."

Lina smiled, closed her eyes, rested her head on him, and cherished Rakesh's warm embrace.

AUTHOR'S NOTE

The Second Phase is a work of fiction. All characters depicted in this book are purely fictional and any similarity to a real person or place is coincidental. I must admit that only a negligible amount of research went into the writing of this book. In other words, my research entailed no more than Google search; nevertheless, I am certainly grateful for the content that I discovered through the search. All remaining contents are either figment of my imagination, or based on what I know. Any omissions or errors are therefore mine only.

Thank you.

San Ika

ABOUT THE AUTHOR

San Ika was born in India and lived in Canada for several years before moving to the United States. He lives in the metropolitan Detroit area with his wife and son. The Second Phase is his first novel.

Made in the USA
Charleston, SC
04 February 2014